Your Sins
and
Mine

Your Sins and Mine

Mine

By
Taylor Caldwell

ÆONIAN PRESS▲

MATTITUCK

DEDICATION
To Richard Carroll with affection

Reprinted 1976 by Special Arrangement

Library of Congress Catalog Card Number 82-72974
International Standard Book Number 0-88411-168-7

To order, contact
Aeonian Press
Box 1200
Mattituck, New York 11952

Manufactured in the United States of America

CHAPTER ONE

MY FATHER was no different from other men; he had the wisdom of hindsight. He was also a countryman, and had never been far from the place where he was born, and had always lived close to the earth. So when he told us later of what he had seen in early January—a few months before the strange and awful things had come to pass— we discounted it as superstition, for he was what used to be called a "fundamentalist."

"Yes," he would say somberly, "it was because all of us everywhere in the world were really strangers—hating strangers—every man to his neighbors and every nation to other nations. It was necessary for us to be punished so that we'd finally see the light. 'For then shall be great tribulation, such as was not since the beginning of the world to this time, now, nor ever shall be.' Matthew 24:21." My father knew his Bible almost by heart.

During the years when the nations of the world stood poised, armed and terrified and hating, my father used to quote Matthew 24 almost daily. His voice would take on an ominous note new to him, for he was naturally a simple and optimistic man. The seasons never failed; God never failed. The sun swung in its fiery orbit, and the green tides of the world rose and fell with it, under the hand of God. That was my father's serene faith. But after the first atomic bombs fell, and the hatred of men became more fierce and more insane, and the hydrogen bombs were invented, then my father's faith in man began to fail.

He was in his middle fifties that January, strong, almost monolithic in stature, ruddy and zestful and full of roaring laughter. He was a graduate of one of the best agricultural colleges in the country, and was known as a student of world affairs. He had once served as mayor of Arbourville Township, and no one I have ever known, before or since, was more aware of what was happening in the world. No, my father was not senile that January, nor was he a few months later when he told us of what he had seen. . . .

Unable to sleep one night, he went out of the house silently, and stood smoking on the hard and frozen brown earth. He had remarked a week before that we had had practically no snow, and this had made him uneasy. But he was certain that this was just another of those vagaries of nature which always plague a farmer's life.

He told us that it had been a very calm, starry night, heavy with stillness. But it was not the customary stillness of a country midnight. It held an ominous quality, as if waiting for something enormously strange to happen. A farm midnight has its own familiar sounds: a horse will neigh, a cow complain, a sleeping dog bark, chickens flutter and flurry in their sheds. Life, though sleeping, is still alive.

My father smoked, his heavy, plaid jacket buttoned to his neck, his feet spread apart on the brown earth in his usual sturdy fashion. It was some time before he became aware of the absolute silence all about him. The barns might have been empty, the fields uninhabited, the woods abandoned. The house behind him held all of us, sleeping, its big whiteness glimmering under a moon

6

that was so bright my father could see the east meadow, where the winter wheat was already green; he could see the woods, the bare black branches of the trees snarled together. He could see the brook which ran like quicksilver, unimpeded by any ice, beyond the barns. And here and there he could see a farmhouse window where a single light shone, testifying to birth or illness.

We should have had snow by now, a lot of it, thought my father. We should have had it in November and December. He looked at the sky again, crowded with stars, and at the great white moon. He studied it all with a countryman's wisdom, searching for a single cloud. It was cold enough for snow; it was very cold.

He recalled that, according to the farm journals, lack of rainfall and snow was causing farmers all over the country considerable uneasiness. No rain of any importance in the South; Texas was drying up. The mighty plains of Iowa and Idaho and Kansas were reporting an alarming lack of moisture of any kind since the first of November. But still, thought my father, this has happened several times in my lifetime, and just when it is needed most desperately rain or snow comes and the crops are in and there's a good harvest, generally.

He was still uneasy, though, and he scowled up at the dry stars and the dry moon. The smoke from his pipe curled up before his face, straight as a stick. He tested the ground with his feet; it was as hard as concrete.

Then, all at once, according to my father, the moon was gone.

He looked up alertly, pleased and expectant. It must be clouding up.

But it was not clouding up. The stars flared into greater brilliance now that the moonlight was gone, and their shadows lay on the cold earth. My father waited; he watched for the moon to emerge.

It did not emerge. Where it had been was a small black roundness in the purplish midnight sky. It was barely perceptible, and had there not been a moon a

7

few moments before my father would not even have
noticed it. It's surely a cloud, just as big as the face of
the moon, he thought, and again he waited. But the
cloud, if it was one, did not move aside, and the stars
glared more feverishly at the earth.

Now the silence had a quality of terror in it. It was
as if the earth had drawn in a great breath, and, with it,
all sound. My father was standing in an absolute vacuum
under the stars. He could not bear it; he stamped his feet
on the ground and the little noise came back to him, flat
and lifeless. It was worse than the silence.

Almost sick with fear, his face upturned, he watched
the sky. He must have watched, he said later, for at least
half an hour. Then he saw a thin curved thread of bright
orange in the hole where the moon had been. Ah, the
cloud was passing. But why was the thread that awe-
some color? It was turning red, like a bent blade fresh
from a tempering fire. With awful slowness it thickened,
became a crescent, then a half, then a full moon. It was
larger than before, and as scarlet as blood. The stars retreated into a diffused pallor.

. . . and the moon shall not give her light, thought my
father, remembering his Bible. The moon, though the
color of blood, and bright, and even larger than a harvest
or a hunter's moon, did not give any light. The earth
was dark.

It was an eclipse, my father thought with a desperation
alien to him. He watched a little longer, until the watching became unendurable. He went back into the house,
and it was not until he felt the warmth inside that he
realized he was very cold, colder than he had ever been in
his life. His hands were so stiff that he had to fumble for a
few moments before he could turn on a lamp in the
parlor. His fingers were rigid and numb. Then he began
to shiver uncontrollably; in his heavy jacket, near the
table where he kept his farm journals. His unyielding
fingers could hardly turn the pages.

No eclipses of the moon were forecast for this time
of the year in this latitude.

The journal dropped from his knees and my father sat on his worn leather chair. He heard the old clock ticking away in the hall outside. The silence that lay over the land blanketed the parlor, and all at once he could no longer hear the clock. He waited, and moisture broke out on his forehead. He glanced at the windows. A fiery glare shone through the Venetian blinds, like the reflection from a burning building.

The barns, thought my father, confusedly. But he knew it was not the barns. Sunken in his chair, he watched the windows. Then he pushed himself to his feet with a supreme effort and went into the hall and switched on the light. He looked at the old walnut clock which had belonged to his grandfather. The pendulum was not moving. The hands stood still at the hour, the chimes were silent.

"I couldn't move, I tell you," my father said to us months later. "I wanted to call one of you boys, but I couldn't. I just sat on the stairs and looked at the clock. At least I couldn't see the moon from there."

He was never quite certain how long he sat huddled on the steps staring at the clock. Perhaps half an hour, perhaps an hour. But all at once he became conscious that the clock was ticking again, feebly, hesitantly at first, then with strong assurance. The chimes sounded the hour of half-past one; then, without a pause, they struck two. The hands on the clock had moved to that hour, as if turned forward by an invisible hand.

The silence of the earth had gone. Now a sleeping horse neighed; one of the dogs barked, another whined. A wind suddenly took the house and shook it gently. My father, trembling again, stood up and went back into the parlor and pulled up the blind on one of the windows. The moon was white and clear and shining in a peaceful sky.

My father picked up his Bible with his cold hands and reread Matthew 24, not once, but many times. It was three o'clock before he climbed the stairs to bed, to lie

9

beside my sleeping mother until dawn lightened the windows. Then he slept, himself.

In the morning he was exhausted. When he came to breakfast I remember that he looked at each of us very strangely, as if seeing us for the first time, and recalling something. But he did not say what he had seen—if he had really seen it and it had not been all a dream—until months later.

There was no report of any of this in the newspapers, which he read that day for the first time in many weeks. He decided he must have dreamed it. . . .

Soon after this we noticed the absence of newspapers and periodicals in the house. My father had stopped all subscriptions. Finally he would not even listen to the radio. He would sit alone in the parlor, his Bible in his hands, and though no son or grandchild had ever before feared to burst in on him at any time, they feared to now. It was as if he had withdrawn from us all for contemplation. Even Mother, to whom he was so devoted, left him alone near the fire, and her face lost its merriment.

But my father was a farmer, after all. We have a fairly large farm, some seven hundred acres, stock and truck. My brother Edward and I had no longings for the city and city life, and from our early youth we had taken it for granted that even when we were married we would remain on the farm. Edward and I had served our time in the Army—I in Korea, he in Europe. We had enlisted. Father had resigned himself to the wars with a country-man's fatalism. After all, there were always the seasons and the sun—and God. They were the eternal verities which man could never destroy.

We had two tenant farmers and their families on the farm, and my father and I ran things with great success. My brother Edward could not help us very much. He had been blinded in Europe in 1945.

Edward had never been blessed—or cursed—with much imagination. He was calm and matter-of-fact, like our mother. He underwent a period of training, and, as he

10

had always had a gift for mechanics, he soon learned how to repair farm machinery. So while he could do little on the land, he kept himself busy and was happy enough. He and his wife Lucy and their two boys occupied two of the large rear bedrooms in the big clapboard house, while Jean and I and our new son had the two front bedrooms.

My father took Edward's blindness philosophically, it seemed, until after I returned from Korea. Then I would see him looking at Edward, and his kind face, so broad and strong, would become tight and he would turn away without speaking. Once, soon after my return, when I was talking about my experiences in prison camp, he said to me: "Yes, we are all strangers to each other, and that's why we hate each other so much and want to kill each other. Pete, don't talk to me about war any more."

At Christmas time we had bought a television set, but we soon learned not to tell Father about the news. He made it plain that he wanted no information. However, he would sometimes say in a voice of new harshness: "Well, how many hydrogen bombs have we, or they, exploded recently? Let me see, Pete, your boy will be ready in about seventeen years, won't he? And yours, Ed, in less than that, eh? Better have some more children quick; we'll need them."

However, he did not neglect his work, and would talk cheerfully enough about crops and cattle. So we thought this bitterness was a phase that would pass.

CHAPTER TWO

A LITTLE RAIN, hard with sleet, fell twice during January. But the brook shrank under shards of ice until it was just a narrow frozen bed. The river near Arbourville fell to the lowest level in its history. There were complaints from all over that the water level was falling and municipal governments were warning people to ration themselves. Texas was as dry as a bone, but then, farmers said to each other, Texas was usually dry. No real concern was felt until the Midwestern states declared an emergency. That was in early February, and even then we were still not really alarmed. We would have a very wet spring, we said to each other.

Washington was silent. No conferences were held; newspapers reported nothing more than an unusual dryness. Rainy England was enjoying "incredibly dry, mild weather," and "the people were taking advantage of it for outings." Italy was warm as summer, and the Riviera, in spite of the increasing threats of war, was crowded. There were gay accounts of hardy Scandinavian bathers taking dips along the beaches, but complaining that they would rather be skiing, if only it would snow. India was

12

suffering a drought, but when did India not suffer a drought?

The spring and early summer rains had not come to South America: November, December, January and February had never been so dry in all recorded history. We did not know then that the great fruit companies in the States were greatly alarmed about tropical crops in the southern republics. From beyond the steel borders of Russia and her satellite countries no news came at all—at first.

Japan was delighted that the much feared spring floods did not appear in February. The Ohio Valley was happy that the river was not swelling. Cincinnati forgot to look at her bridges, and reveled in the extraordinarily warm sunlight. Men swarmed about the lower reaches of the Mississippi River and rejoiced that this year they would not have to shore up the levees.

It was not until much later that we learned that the oases in the deserts everywhere had sifted into endless sands, the palms filtering into dust, the green places shriveling and blowing off under a sun that was never dimmed. Later, too, we learned of the retreating seas which shrank from the earth, and the rivers which dwindled more and more.

But this was all much later, as you remember. There were as yet few signs of what was to come.

My father had a special devotion to trees. A tree against a glittering orange sunset was, to him, the most beautiful thing in the world. He would walk among the trees in the summer and touch their leaves and talk to them as one would talk to a dear child. Perhaps the trees responded, for we had the best in the township, never dying off, never afflicted with disease, always thickening, always bearing.

It was my father's custom, toward the end of February, to visit the orchards and some of his favorite trees, such as the enormous clump of elms on the knoll beyond the south meadow, the maples at the border of

13

Mother's garden, the white birches near the gate and the Normandy poplar far up beyond the wheat fields.

This 25th of February he came into our warm old brick kitchen ready for his customary first walk to the orchards. Each year since Edward had returned home blind, my father had merely come into the kitchen and indicated with a movement of his head that he wished me to accompany him, and I would get up and follow as quietly as possible. But this morning my father, who had, for some weeks, seemed especially tired and withdrawn, said: "Ed—Pete—I'm going to visit the trees. Come along." My mother turned sharply from the stove with sudden tears in her eyes, and Lucy, Edward's wife, uttered a faint exclamation.

It was a fine, clear day, full of pale sunlight and very still. When Edward turned his blind eyes toward my father a beam of light illuminated his face and I saw an expression of pain on it. "George," said my mother, very gently. Lucy's mouth trembled, and when she glanced at my father it was with sternness.

My father was silent for a moment, and then he said quietly, "I'm sorry. I'd forgotten. Come on, Pete."

I did not believe he had forgotten, and I was puzzled and angry. My father was the kindest and most considerate of men, and this behavior was not like him at all. He walked out of the room in his heavy boots and I followed. I glanced back at Edward. He was just sitting there, his hands on the table, his head bent. Edward was a thin, brown young man, soft-spoken and easy in manner. We had become accustomed to the blurred glasses he wore, but now all at once I saw them as if seeing them for the first time, and I was shocked to the heart. I closed the kitchen door quietly behind me, sick with compassion for my brother—and my father.

The parched and sullen earth lay before us, and it came keenly to me that the lawns about the house were showing no grass except in little yellowish patches. I looked far in the distance to the jade stand of wheat, and was mysteriously comforted. My father was moving quickly now, and I hurried to catch up with him. He stopped at the maples, and looked at them. The buds were swelling and turning to a dim rose, and he touched them gently. We went to the white beeches, and there too the buds glimmered frostily. Then, still without exchanging a word, we walked to the elms, whose tight buds were showing the faintest green. We went into the fruit orchards, and for the first time my father spoke to me. "In another three weeks, they'll be in flower."

Then, abruptly, he was silent. He had taken hold of a gnarled apple branch and he was looking at it intently. I joined him, for he had become rigid and his usually highly colored face had grayed. Speechlessly, he moved the branch towards me. There were no buds on it. My father moved to the next tree and the next, and I trailed him, our shadows following us on the brown earth. There were no buds at all on any of the apple trees. I broke a twig, and the wood was green. I did not know how constricted my throat had become until I tried to speak. I had to swallow a few times before I could say, "Well, it's been a dry winter, but the trees are alive, and so—"

"And so," said my father, and his voice trembled. He went on and all at once it seemed to me there was a queer emptiness in the cold February light. Perhaps it was my father's face, so barren of expression except for his eyes, which had a bitter grimness in them, as if he knew something I did not.

Again we were silent, as we went to the cherry orchard. We examined tree after tree, not speaking. We went to the peach orchard, and to the pear. There was not a single flower bud on any tree, and time after time I broke twigs to see the living green in them.

We stood and looked at each other. My father said, "You remember that we lost all our female calves this year, and only a few of the young bulls lived."

"Yes," I said. "And it's happened to all our neighbors. There are practically no milch cows in this whole area."

"Our hens are laying only a few eggs, and none of them has been fertilized." My father turned to me and

15

stared at me long and somberly. "Do you think this is just local? It's been reported all over the country. 'Dryness.' "

"What do you say, Dad?" I asked.

But he only shook his head and gazed at the sky.

We went to the winter wheat, but as we approached it we saw it had lost much of its greenness, and when we stood among it we could see that it was dying.

When we returned to the house I was shivering. My father went to the telephone and called the Grange office in Arbourville. He spoke very little, and asked a few questions. Then he hung up and turned to me. "Yes, it's all over the state. None of the fruit trees are showing buds, and there are reports of wheat dying from the Pacific to the Atlantic. The Florida crop was almost nothing. There isn't enough wheat or lettuce or any other kind of vegetable to ship, and though they've gathered a good harvest of oranges the trees aren't showing any flowers."

"We'll have to irrigate," I said. We stood in the hall, and suddenly I had to sit down on one of the chairs lined against the wall. I remembered the reports of the sinking rivers, and I also remembered that our well's level was dropping and the pump was working almost constantly.

"We've never had to irrigate," my father said, and his voice had lost its strength. "We've always had enough rainfall. We're not prepared to irrigate, and neither are our neighbors." He added, as if to himself, "It would do no good, anyway."

"Why not?" I asked helplessly.

But my father did not answer. I noticed that he was staring strangely at the clock, but as he had not told us yet what he had seen—or dreamed—I could not understand that strange look.

He went out of the house again and I followed like a child. We found Edward in the barn tinkering with the engine of one of the plows. He heard us come in and

16

lifted his head alertly. My father went to him and put his hand on my brother's shoulder. "You're being avenged, Ed," he said. "The whole world forgot you, but God has remembered."

CHAPTER THREE

THE NEWSPAPERS, even the country weeklies, seemed to ignore the farmers. The farm journals, too, were curiously silent. Now we know that Washington had directed them not to print the things that were happening. A panic was feared, not so much in the country as in the cities. Perhaps Washington was right. Cities panic easily.

Washington was silent. Congress met and discussed the possible amounts of atomic and hydrogen bombs which Russia was producing. They talked of allies and human rights and investigations into the drug traffic and the future of the United Nations. They talked of everything except what was uppermost in their minds.

And all the time the earth stood barren, except for the fruitless trees, and the ground dried and blew in brown storms over the land. There was not a word from the other capitals of the world, and not a word, as yet, from Russia. There was just one significant trend which millions of readers passed over in their newspapers: belligerence was beginning to disappear from among the delegates to the United Nations, and talk was abstract and muted. Even the mention of new land and sea bases for the Western allies aroused not a single angry comment from the Russians. In fact, they made no comment at all.

We heard, much later, that the "bread basket" of Russia—the Ukraine—was producing no wheat, and that the endless collectivized farms were as hard-packed and fruitless as ours were. Everywhere in the world the land refused to bear fruit. But for now a conspiracy of silence hung over the world.

And the sun shone, cloudless, in the sky, and the rivers dropped and the seas shrank and the creeks and brooks dried up and the mountains were sear and the valleys yellowed—all over the world.

The land hated us, the violated land, the faithful land, the exploited and gentle land. The land had decided that we must die, and all innocent living things with us. The land had cursed us. Our wars and our hatred—these had finally sickened the wise earth.

We did not know then that we stood indicted as the enemy of life. . . .

It was the end of February, and in our part of the country the weather was as fair and gentle as May. We awoke every morning to calm and relentless sunshine. The trees brightened daily into thickening green, and even the fruit trees, though never showing a single flower, sprang into leaf. But the corn did not sprout; the meadows lay in hot brownness under the polished sky, giving birth only to prickly weeds inedible for man and beast. Some weeds which had disappeared years ago under constant cultivation had unaccountably returned and were definitely poisonous, so that we kept our large flocks out of the fields. We did not allow them even to go to the water holes, for they had long since dried. They had been sucked into the earth, as if suddenly gulped down by some subterranean giant.

We had considerable hay stored in our barns, and

19

feed in the silos; we fed the cattle as we fed them during the winter. But for some reason the cattle did not thrive. They were restless in the sunshine, and complained, and their flesh dwindled. The few calves we had had in the winter sickened and died. The cow's milk diminished until we had only enough for ourselves, a thin, bluish fluid which produced almost no butter.

"Well," said my father, with that grim humor which was now almost a permanent characteristic of his, "the Government will have to disgorge those millions of pounds of butter they've been buying from the farmers and put it on the market. I've noticed the grocery stores are having sales on it, at low prices, too. Keeping the cities quiet, I suppose."

The Government not only disgorged its butter but began to disgorge the bursting warehouses of the wheat it had bought from the farmers. But we did not know that for some time. Nor did we know that all exports of wheat had been halted. We learned nothing in the newspapers of the millions dying of famine in India and Asia.

My brother Edward said nothing. He worked on the farm machinery, though he knew his work was useless. His hands slowed and a strange stillness lay on his face. Perhaps it was because our children, fed with that thin, bluish milk, gained little weight and cried almost constantly. At night I would lie beside my wife, Jean, and listen hopelessly. And Jean, who had always been bright and full of laughter, would weep soundlessly, believing me asleep. The moonlight would make a clear black pool of her hair on the pillow, and I would want to touch it. But if I did she would know I was frightened and then it would be worse for her.

The Grange did not call any extra meetings in Arbourville to discuss what was happening. We know now that they had received their orders, as all the Granges had received them, from Washington. But on the first of March they called their regular meeting, and my father and I attended with the other farmers in the area.

I was horrified when I saw Lester Hartwick, our local president. I had seen him last in January, a happy, jocose farmer, as colorful as a ripe pear, as short and bulky as a boulder. He had become an old man in two months, shriveled and wasted, his flesh as gray as his thick hair. He opened the meeting as matter-of-factly as usual and shuffled papers on the table. Then he looked up at us and his gaze was absent and clouded.

"Well, fellows," he said, "we've been having bad luck this spring with our crops. Not having had—much—rain and such. But it's still only March, and we can expect rain any day." He faltered, stopped, and bent his head over the table.

Then my father stood up.

"Les," he said, "you know damn well we aren't going to have any rain. And don't tell me it's just in this area. It's all over the world, and you know it."

"Now, George," said Lester, but he shifted his eyes. "How can you know that? Oh, sure, there's a drought in Texas, but they've been having droughts for years—"

"I know the newspapers aren't printing anything," said my father, "and neither are the farm journals. But I know what's happening all over the world. How do I know?" He pointed at his chest. "Something tells me, in here. Who's been warning you Grange presidents to keep quiet?"

Lester laughed; it was a feeble sound. "George, you sound like a prophet of doom. You know as well as I do that some years the crops are light, but the next year—"

"There probably won't be a next year for most of us," said my father. The farmers were looking steadily at him now, and not at Lester Hartwick. "We've got just one court of appeals now," my father said, "and I don't suppose most of you have given it any thought. Oh, I suppose you've prayed for rain, in church. But have you ever prayed: 'God have mercy on me, a sinner,' like the publican in the Bible? I guess you haven't; your faces are the answer. I wonder how many of you even know your Bible? I wonder how many of you know we're all being

21

punished, and that we've had a sentence of death handed to us?"

At first some of the men in the room smiled uneasily at my father's words, but soon the smiles faded and they gave him all their attention. He was big and powerful as he stood there, with his grave and somber face illuminated by the spring sunlight.

"Yes, a sentence of death," he said, with authority. "Because every man in the world is a sinner against every other man, and against God. It isn't only all the wars we've had in this century. We've forgotten God."

My father tightened his belt and ran his hand over the stubble on his chin. His blue eyes were vivid—vivid and condemning—as they traveled slowly over every face in the room.

"I'm no politician. I'm a farmer, just as you are. When we were little fellows we took it seriously when the parsons told us we owed a duty to our fellow man, and that the things of the spirit are more important than the things of the body. Every church told its people that; every church still does, though mostly the parsons speak to empty rows. We don't hear these things with our ears any more. Why? Because every one of us has come to believe that the things of the body are the only valuable things, and we've scrambled for them over the rights of all other men. We've become too materialistic, too atheistic. Look, I'm no orator. You know what I'm talking about.

"And now we shake our atomic and hydrogen bombs in Russia's face and she shakes hers in ours, and we both go on exploding them over the land and destroying it. But war is a profitable thing. It's what makes cities grow and thrive."

My father's eyes flashed over the listening faces of the men. "In my father's day the people were happy on the land. Men raised food, not factories for the weapons of murder. Sure, maybe we didn't all have big cars in our barns, and gadgets in our houses, but an oil lamp does just

22

as well as electricity, and a book is better than some of the stuff we see on television.

"What has all our progress brought us? Has it brought us peace and safety and love and contentment? No. It has taught us only war. It has taught us to envy our brothers. It has taught us to want more than our brothers. That's materialism; that's hate. There's no place on God's earth for materialism and hate and godlessness and war. That's why we've been sentenced to death."

He lifted one of his big hands, slowly and solemnly. "The earth will live. She isn't going to allow us to destroy her with our bombs. She's just going to get rid of the monsters who might, some day very soon, send her spinning airless and fruitless through space, or blow her into dust. The earth knows God, and God is with the earth. She's stood our antics too long; she suffered, and she was kind. Now we are going to die, for we've gone too far in our hate and greed."

He raised his head and cried out, "May God have mercy on our souls!"

Like a mighty chorus to his words there answered the rolling sound of spring thunder, and all at once the sun was gone and the light in the room became gray. The farmers started to their feet, and looked at the windows.

Lester Hartwick laughed with delight and shouted, "Look, it's going to rain at last! George, you old Jeremiah, it's going to rain!"

And rain it did. Suddenly the windows were silvery cataracts and lightning blazed and thunder shook the air. The street outside disappeared in the torrents; through some partly opened window gushed the scent of wet dust and the freshness of life. The farmers shouted with relief and joy, and slapped my father's back and talked deliriously about being able to set the crops now.

The rain poured down and we watched it, crowding to the windows. The dried brooks would run now, and the rivers would rise. I looked at my father, but he was not smiling. He said: "The earth won't die. The rain will

23

save the fruitless trees, but it's too late for the fruitful ones. The sentence of death is still with us."

We heard, over the radio that night, that rain was falling all over the world in gushing floods. And for the first time we learned that the drought had been worldwide.

It rained for many days, and the farmers plowed joyously in it and sang, and set their crops, and held up their faces to the dark and pouring heavens. All over the world it rained, and the cruel sun was gone for a long time. The forests freshened and the rivers tumbled everywhere.

But the wheat did not come up, and the fruit trees, though green as jade, did not put out any flowers, and the inundated earth did not brighten with grass. It remained lifeless except for bursting acres of poisonous weeds. Vegetables did not grow, though flowers bloomed everywhere—flowers which men and beasts could not eat.

CHAPTER FOUR

When we arrived home on that first day of rain, Jean ran to me and said: "Pete, the birds have come back!"

We men had not noticed that the birds had disappeared, for we had been too desperate. But when I looked through the parlor window I saw that the brown earth was full of robins and blackbirds and other migratory creatures. They were very busy, pulling worms from the ground and shrilling in the wet twilight and hopping about with a kind of feverish activity. Somehow the very sight of them heartened me and my private terror diminished.

The water holes had reappeared, but we could not let the cattle go to them. As if some evil force had willed it, we saw that the weeds were thickening, thrusting out strange yellow and red flowers and enormous thorns. They crowded about the water holes, poisoning them. That night we led the cattle to the hurrying brook and let them drink their fill, and we stood about them with heavy sticks for fear that they would try to eat the weeds. But we did not need to keep them away. They

25

looked at the weeds with as much fear as we did, and huddled together to avoid even stepping on them.

The rains went on. When they stopped for an hour or so there was a curious stench on the earth. It hung like a deadly fog in the air. We went out to find its source. The weeds were exuding it, and as we came closer to them—they were pushing up over our lawns now as well as in the fields—the smell choked us and forced us to cover our noses. It was the very essence of corruption. We could see the colors of these monstrous flowers and their dark green thorny leaves as far as our eyes could reach. When, after a week or so, the long barbed tendrils reached up to our windows, waving like tentacles, Jean cried out in horror, and she and my mother and Lucy gathered the children about them, cradling them with their bodies.

Ten of our best cows died one night, after the weeds had reached the walls of our house and our barns. Half of our chickens died, without reason. Two of our horses sickened, and expired before morning. The pigs looked at their troughs and turned away. We could see the ribs on their gaunt bodies.

The newspapers mentioned casually that there had been an infestation of weeds "in this area." (We did not know then that these weeds had appeared in every country all over the world.) "However," said a spokesman, "plowing and vigorous cultivation will destroy them. Botanists are baffled. Samples are being rushed to Washington. But it is just in this area."

In early April a tremendous hydrogen bomb was exploded in the Southwest. There were pictures of it in the newspapers. Washington boasted that it was the biggest bomb ever to be exploded, and the military were jubilant. They were certain Russia had no comparable bomb of her own.

The Russians were silent. The whole earth was silent. No nation permitted the news of the weeds and the deathly smell to extend beyond its borders.

Then, without warning, the President, on a radio

26

broadcast, pleaded with the people not to travel "more than necessary." Rubber was in "short supply" and so was gasoline.

"Lies, lies," said my father. "Washington wants to prevent the people from seeing what is happening in other states besides their own."

There was talk of rationing if the people did not co-operate. A week later an emergency was declared, and the people were warned that those driving for pleasure over the country would be penalized ". . . until rubber and gasoline, needed now for defense, are again in ample supply."

The warehouses of wheat were rapidly being emptied. Only canned or hothouse vegetables appeared on the market, and the people complained of the prices. They did not complain too much, however, for butter was very cheap. Milk had become exorbitant, and mothers wrote tens of thousands of letters to Washington, and received no reply. "The farmers are greedy; they are holding back the milk for higher prices!" cried the city mothers, looking at their pale children. The farm mothers were silent. They knew there was little or no milk. The Government urged the women to use the millions of cans of evaporated milk on the shelves of their grocery stores "until milk is in good supply again," it pleaded. There had been a drought all over the country, Washington explained, and cattle were not producing the product "adequately."

"And when the evaporated milk is gone—what then?" asked my father. But we did not answer.

The newspapers reported that the rains had "come just in time to save the crops." The fact that there were no crops was kept a secret. The newspapers filled their pages with accounts of the United Nations. "There seems to be emerging a new calm and a faint sign of a willingness to co-operate on the part of Russia." A Communist Polish delegate stood up and announced that there were no problems in the world which could not be settled by "peaceful negotiation." He was applauded even

27

by the Russian delegates, who had lately lost their scowls.

We saw that all the photographed faces around the crowded diplomatic tables were singularly subdued, that delegates played with pencils and papers and looked about them with haggard glances. Only a few of us detected fear in their eyes; only a few saw the mute questions in those eyes which asked if other nations were enduring the same plague. No one, of course, answered.

One day a Russian delegate rose to his feet to express "the People's Democracies' " sympathy for the suffering of India, "which has experienced the worst drought in its history." The People's Democracies would ship to India millions of tons of wheat in the immediate future. In fact, ships were already on their way. The Ukraine, said the Russian delegate, with a happy smile, was bursting with new wheat. Crops would be the largest in history.

"Liar! Liar!" said my father, grimly. "There will be some wheat shipped, yes. Russia wants the world to believe that only she has not been struck down. Some wheat—but only a little—from their warehouses. After that, nothing."

He was right, of course. Later we heard that the farmers on the collective farms were fighting government agents in a frantic attempt to keep some of their corn for themselves, and some of their cattle. But that was much later.

In the middle of April a new stench added itself to the awful one which was always with us. The wild creatures in the woods were dying rapidly, poisoned by the weeds. Deer and rabbits and squirrels and woodchucks and mice littered the floor of the forests, decaying.

Then the birds began to die.

It was about that time that my father told us what he had seen in January. We listened to him intently. Then he read to us from Matthew 24.

We did not know at that time that millions of Bibles were being opened all over the world, and that churches

28

were beginning to burst with new members. But the ministers did not speak of what was happening all over the country. They, too, had been given their orders.

Fear hung over the world like a vast cloud.

CHAPTER FIVE

MY MOTHER was a very amiable, gentle woman, round and pink as an apple, with warm brown eyes and pretty chestnut hair which curled all about her face in tiny ringlets. She was a great favorite in our part of the country, for she was completely without malice or smallness of character. She could silence an outburst of my father's with a slight glance or a faint smile, and I cannot remember that she was ever impatient. Lucy and Jean loved her, and her little grandsons followed her everywhere. She was never too tired to listen to anyone, and her calmness had the quality of the earth in it.

It was some time before we noticed that her color had faded and that her hair was whitening about the temples and that she was silent now, rather than calm. One night in May she said to my father: "We used to have so many visitors on Saturdays and Sundays. No one comes any more."

We had lived with fear for so many weeks that we were all startled into this new awareness of the absence of friends. The telephone hardly rang these days. The roads were empty, and the matted weeds were running their tentacles across them. Our driveway was snarled with them; they grew together, piled up on themselves and in many places they reached a height of three feet. There was no place now which was not infested with them. But though in furious red and yellow bloom, no bee approached them. They strangled my mother's flower garden, crawled up fences and tree trunks, wound themselves about posts. We kept our stock in the barns, huddled together, and the doors shut to keep out that silent rage of death. They darkened our windows and gushed across our porch. Sometimes at night, when a strong wind blew, we could hear them rustle harshly.

There were no school children in our house, but we heard that the schools in the county had been closed. A few children's legs had been pierced by the thorns and they had almost died of the poisoning.

We had heard nothing as yet about the cities, and it was not until summer that we did hear from friends who had visited there that the city parks were overrun with the horror which could not be exterminated. But the streets themselves remained clear because of the traffic.

We were a reserved family, not given to hysteria or panic. The women might sit, white-faced, with the children on their knees, but when they spoke it was with their usual quietness. It was very difficult for them, for the children could not be allowed out and they were restless as well as half sick from the want of sunshine and milk.

At first only my father believed that we had been condemned to death with all our fellows. Edward and I sometimes laughed wearily together about his dream of the moon and the stopping of time. But as the endless days went by, our laughter faded and we did not speak of that "dream."

One night my mother suddenly cried out in a strange voice: "George, what can we do? The children—the children—"

"We can do nothing," answered my father bitterly.

31

He went to her and put his arms about her and we heard her sobbing against his chest. "The children have been condemned with us."

"But they're so innocent," wept my mother.

"But so many millions of innocents have already been murdered," my father said. He looked at us over my mother's head and quoted again from the Bible: "The voice of thy brother's blood crieth unto me from the ground. And now thou art cursed from the earth. . . ."

I thought of Korea, and Edward, sitting near me in his blindness, turned toward my father. He said, quietly, "Yes, I killed men. I had no choice."

"And I had no choice," I added.

Edward put his hands over his face and for the first time I heard him quote the Bible too: "My punishment is greater than I can bear."

My mother lifted her head from my father's chest and looked at us aghast, her eyes swollen with tears. "But it was Cain who said that, Edward!"

My brother and I did not answer her.

My mother turned to my father, exclaiming: "What could our boys do? Did they make those wars?"

"Yes," said my father. "We all did."

I got up abruptly and left the room, for suddenly I hated my father for what I believed to be his cruelty. I stood in the hall, trembling, and Jean came out to me and put her arms around me. I had no comfort for her. I could only stand there with my hands clenched. A sense of impotent rage came over me, a hatred and disgust for all the world, for my father, and then, strangely, for myself. I was swamped in my emotions, my feeling of helplessness and despair.

And then, like a tolling in my inner ear, came the awful words: *It repented the Lord that He had made man on the earth . . . The earth mourneth and fadeth away . . . The earth also is defiled under the inhabitants thereof; because they have transgressed the laws . . . Therefore hath the curse devoured the earth. . . .*

I pushed Jean away from me roughly. "Surely to God

there must be something we can do!" I cried. "Why doesn't the government send out armies of men to kill the damned things?"

I walked away from Jean and went upstairs to our room and looked at our sleeping baby. . . .

When Jean followed me later I pretended to be asleep. She moved about quietly by the light of one small lamp. She sank onto the bed beside me and I could feel her sobbing silently to herself again. I turned and took her in my arms and kissed her, and for a little while, in our love, we forgot that we had been condemned to die.

Jean slept, but I could not. I saw the blanched white face of the moon peering in the window, and I thought of its barrenness. I hated it. I got up and pulled the curtains across it. The room was stifling in the June heat, but we dared not open the windows because of the choking stench outside. As the hours passed I thought of the cities and the land, and wondered how long it would be before every sign of man had been smothered in death.

I turned and tossed in the heat of the room and the thought of the weeds, the dreadful weeds, became an obsession. They were no longer a vegetable manifestation of some unknown evil or judgment, but a sinister purpose, animated, directed. I wanted to fight that purpose; I wanted to show that I could combat it.

When the first signs of dawn turned the windows gray I got up and dressed. I crept down the dark staircase and listened to the monotonous song of the old clock. Then I was outside, my legs protected by high leather boots. I passed through the weeds and they snatched at me with their long barbs and ripped at my clothing. I held my arms high from them, and they seethed about my legs, hungrily. They crackled under my feet, and I breathed shallowly through my nose to keep from being stifled by their stench. I could not see them in the darkness, but I could feel their baleful life, their awareness of me, their hatred for me.

Above me, the eastern sky streamed with pale magenta light, streaked with cold green. I reached the barns and had to wrench open the doors with all my strength, for in a single night the weeds had overrun the hinges. The barns were very warm, for our animals were huddled there—those which remained of the flocks we had once owned. The cows did not stamp or complain; even when I lit a lantern they merely looked at me with the mute eyes of despair. "Quiet, quiet," I murmured to them, and they lowered their heads. The three horses sighed gustily. I went from stall to stall, offering comfort to these poor creatures, touching them. Our two remaining bulls nuzzled me, young fellows who only a month ago would have bellowed and tossed their horns. "It's all right, boys," I said to them, stroking their broad shoulders. They moved nearer to me, and I knew that never again would I regard any poor beast as a mere commodity to be fattened and sent to the market.

My hatred for the weeds reached a frantic pitch in my mind, for now I finally understood how they would stifle the innocent as well as the guilty. I must do something! I went outdoors and stood irresolute. The hills in the distance, which should have been a soft lavender in the dawn light, were venomous in color.

I moved toward another building. The weeds tried to seize me and pull me down. I tore among them, crushing my heels into them savagely, but they sprang up behind me as I hurried. I reached the building where we kept our farm machinery, and the fury in me grew wilder. I climbed onto the seat of our huge disk harrow, whose edges were as sharp as knives. I drove out through the weeds. The disks cut them; I could hear the edges tearing through the monstrous growth. Now it was light enough to see that they were bleeding, a green, noxious blood which spewed up about me like a deathly water. The smell was overpowering, but there was a sort of mad rejoicing in me. Surely I was killing them with the harrow!

And then I looked behind me. The path of crushed weeds I expected to see had been obliterated. I had made no impression on the weeds at all. Where I had killed, or

34

cut, others now swarmed. I could actually see the movement of them, and it was like a nightmare. The embracing tentacles meshed together visibly.

But I could not stop myself. I drove far into a field, choking on the stench, and the weeds closed eagerly after me. Then, as the first red edge of the sun appeared over the matted hills, I stopped and sat motionless, overcome with futility and anguish.

I was all alone in that monstrous sea. In the distance our house and outbuildings were emerging like faint mirages. Soon my father and the tenant farmers would be going to the barns to set the milking machines hopelessly, and to feed the stock. I sat in the wilderness and began to sob dryly. I put my head on my knees. What was there to do? There was nothing to do. Except to pray.

I sat very still. Pray. I had not prayed since I was a child. I had not been in a church more than three times since I was sixteen.

Surely, I thought, millions must be praying for deliverance from the weeds. What had those prayers accomplished? I looked up at the sky which had become opalescent like the inside of a shell, and I thought bitterly, Where was God that He had permitted this frightful thing to come upon His children? Why, if there was a God—

At least, I thought with infuriated cynicism, I could try prayer. But I could not remember the Our Father beyond the first few words. Now my mind tumbled with meaningless words. I remembered a phrase my father had quoted a few nights ago: *The land shall be utterly emptied, and utterly spoiled.* I lifted my fists to the sky and shouted. "Why, You up there? Why?"

Then I remembered that the prophecy that had been made because of the evil of all men: *I have spoken unto them, but they have not heard* . . . "I'm listening!" I shouted at the sky. "Answer me!"

The weeds rustled harshly in the morning wind. Now there were tears on my face, and anger and hopelessness in my heart. "All right," I said aloud, "there is no—" I heard a voice in my inner ear, saying: *The fool hath said in his heart, There is no God.*

I was overcome. I crouched on the seat and covered my eyes so that I could not see the weeds. Something was stirring in me. Memories were flooding back. I had not been exactly a bad man, only a heedless one, concerned exclusively with my family and the farm, driving hard bargains when I could, killing when I had to, hating when directed. All at once I loathed myself, loathed the meaningless life I had led, loathed my casual obedience to the laws of war.

I too had a share in the crimes against humanity. I looked at the sky again, not with rage, but with despairing humility. I cried out: "Lord, be merciful to me, a sinner!"

The sky, flaming now, was silent; the wind had dropped. The weeds no longer rustled their poisonous song of vengeance. I listened for the birds, but there was never such a silence. I repeated over and over from the very depths of my soul: "Lord, be merciful to me, a sinner."

My hands dropped wearily on the wheel. I must go back to help my father in his useless work. And then, as I turned the wheel, I stopped, incredulous. For the space of about ten yards around the harrow the weeds had retreated. The bare earth lay there, exposed to the first sun, not baked or brown or dry, but warm and crumbling with fertility. "No!" I shouted. I forced myself down to the ground and picked up a handful of soil, still disbelieving. It filtered through my fingers, alive and vital. And I saw that it was meshed with the roots of living grass.

"Oh, God!" I sobbed. "Oh, God!"

What had I said in my jumbled prayers to cause this miracle? I stood, numbed, and tried to remember. It escaped me. There had been a whole torrent of angry prayers. Which one, God, which one? If there had been a special one—

A voice called to me in the silence: "Hey! Hey, you there, Pete!"

I turned slowly toward the fence which separated our land from our neighbor's. It was Johnny Carr, a tall and lanky man of fifty, who had been my father's one and only enemy. He was a jaunty man with a derisive laugh, a thin, dark face and little cunning eyes. Years ago, he and my father had had a bitter boundary dispute, and Carr had won. There had been hostility between the two men ever since, and it had spread to his two sons and to Edward and me.

He stood there now, leaning on the fence, high boots on his long legs, his hat pushed back on his head. He was not grinning, as usual; he was very pale and sober. He was so changed I hardly recognized him. I could not speak, and he vaulted over the fence and came toward me, smiling almost humbly. "These weeds are hell, aren't they, Pete?" he said. His voice was hoarse and friendly, and he peered at me, as if pleading. "What're we going to do? I tried burning them, but it was no good."

Then he saw the empty patch all around the tractor. I heard him take a sharp breath and his face turned as gray as old linen. I watched him in silence. As I had done, he bent and picked up a handful of earth, and examined it lovingly. He looked at me, and his eyes were full of tears. "Oh, Lord," he whispered. "What did you do, Pete?"

"I don't know, Johnny," I said, and my voice was soft. "I think I prayed."

He looked at me dumbly, the fresh warm earth sifting through his fingers. "You prayed?" he stammered at last.
"Yes."

He picked up another handful of earth, and I thought to myself that I no longer resented him. I was sorry for him, sorry for his greed and his cruelty and his hatred for my father. He was suffering as we were all suffering. He might have been a friend, if we had tried to make him one.

He was swallowing painfully. He stared at the weeds,

37

which had been driven back in that wide circle. "Prayed," he muttered. "I never prayed in my life. Never learned how. Nobody taught me." He turned and said: "I was an orphan kid in the county home. Guess there was just too many of us, and then there was the depression. The county just hardly kept us alive. Then I got a job in a machine shop in the city, and when I had a little cash I put it down on my farm—hell of a lot of years before I paid for it. Nobody ever taught me to pray. Never went to church. What for? Kind of foolish, it seemed to me."

He retreated into his thoughts for a moment. Then, "Guess I was hard on my boys," he said. "Never sent them to church. They don't know about praying either. Hard kind of life for all of us; in the early days I kept the boys home from school; just didn't have the money to buy them shoes and clothing. Pete, what did you pray?"

He raised his eyes to me in the full light of the morning, and they brimmed with seeking. "You think maybe there's a God, Pete? You think He maybe cares for me?"

"Yes," I said, and I was surprised at the certainty in my voice. "He cares for all of us."

He took off his wide-brimmed hat and shook his head. "How could He like a man like me, Pete? Sure, I had it hard, and I did hard things; I got into the habit of it. Money was something I didn't see much of until I got that job when I was fifteen. Worked ten hours a day, six days a week. So when I bought the farm, and then the money began to come in, I wanted to hold on to it. Didn't care how I got it. I guess I was scared. Pete, you say you know God cares for me, too?"

I nodded, unable to speak. He leaned against the harrow and studied me with that strange humility. "You do think there's a God, Pete?" Again I nodded. Hesitatingly he held out his hand to me, and I shook it.

"Then why the devil did He send these damn weeds to kill us?"

"I don't know. You'll have to ask my dad. He seems to have the answer." We laughed together, softly.

"Say," he said, "I'm coming right over and talk with your dad. And, say, we got a good milch cow, and no children at home these days. I'll bring the cow over, for your kids." He scratched his chin. "What did you pray, Pete?"

"I told you, I don't remember which prayer it was, Johnny. When I do I'll tell you."

But he was pointing at the weedless patch, and his hand was shaking. I looked where he was pointing. A faint and lovely green was spreading slowly over the vital earth; you could see the grass grow under your very eyes.

CHAPTER SIX

THE MINISTER of my parents' church was a young man, Mr. Warfield Herricks. He was about thirty-two, a year or so older than I, the son of a prosperous farmer. He had the muscles and frame of a hard-working country-man, and the fresh face of a schoolboy. He had served his time as a chaplain in the Army, and those years had not obliterated the bright hope in his gray eyes. Neverthe-less, as he sat now in our parlor, he was troubled.

"I am the last one in the world to deny the power of faith, the power of prayer," he said slowly. "But Pete— well, Pete, you never seemed the kind of a fellow to have any religion; you never came to church—" He hesitated, helplessly. "I never saw you there with your parents."

"I was wrong," I answered, somewhat impatiently.

He became grave. He looked at my parents, at my brother, at Lucy and Jean, and then at Johnny Carr.

"Maybe I'm not very bright, Mr. Herricks," Johnny said. "But even if Pete hasn't been to church lately, what's that got to do with him saying a prayer, and the

40

prayer being answered? Look, I know a lot of folks who go to church regular, and I wouldn't trust them with a barrel of lard. They could pray their heads off and—God—" he faltered and blushed—"wouldn't hear a blasted word of it. Pete, here, prayed and he got answered, and I guess you're kind of mad, in a way, that all your own prayers didn't kill a single weed."

"Don't talk to the parson that way, Johnny," said my father, and tried not to smile.

But Mr. Herricks said simply, "I deserved that, I suppose. Yes, I prayed for the end of the visitation; I had faith." He smiled. "I've heard that even among the saints there is a kind of jealousy."

"Did you have faith that we'd be able to get rid of the weeds and plant crops again?" asked Johnny Carr, staring at our minister.

"Of course, eventually." The young man was obviously unhappy. "After all, it's just a local thing."

"It is?" said Johnny. "I've got friends all over the country; met 'em at stock shows. I raise prize bulls, and we keep writing to each other. Know what they've been writing lately? The weeds are all over. They heard from relatives in Canada, too, that there's the weeds there. Keeping it all quiet, though God knows why."

Then my father told the minister what he had seen in January. Mr. Herricks listened politely and tried not to show his incredulity. He was more unhappy than ever, though he made no remark. Then my father asked pointedly: "Have you read Matthew Twenty-four lately, Mr. Herricks?"

Mr. Herricks was what was known among our simpler neighbors as an educated minister. He had been graduated from one of the more famous divinity colleges in the country, and he was much concerned in his sermons with ethical and social problems. He was almost embarrassed at my father's question, and before he could reply my father went on somberly: "It seems as though a lot of you younger parsons consider the Bible a fine

41

collection of poetry and folk literature—a frame of reference, as they say. You talk politics in your pulpit; you give lectures, and not sermons. You discuss the education of children, the place of women in society, civil liberties, the merits of good citizenship and so on. Now, I'm not saying these aren't important things, you understand. We do need good schools, and we do need women taking more interest in politics and community affairs, and minorities should have their just rights, and nobody should hate his neighbor because he's black or brown or green or red or has another religion other than his own."

He pointed his pipe at the minister. "Good things, all of them. But I say also that you should save them for the parish hall, or the Wednesday night parish meetings. That's the time for lectures. I don't want to hurt your feelings, my boy, but I've noticed that the only time you mention the name of God is when you pray and give the benediction. What do people go to church for, after five or six days of struggling to make a living and worrying about their families and being confused about the world? I can tell you this, they don't go to hear a fine, polished lecture. They go for consolation; they go to be reconciled with God; they go to be assured that God loves them and is waiting to receive their love. They want to know that above the sound and fury of this infernal world there is an everlasting peace, a love that never fails, a mercy that is full of understanding. They want their souls refreshed, not their tired minds belabored."

Mr. Herricks said nothing, but he looked at my father with pain in his eyes.

"Do you believe in miracles?" asked my father, bluntly. "In other words, do you think that God is still capable of performing them or do you think He's sort of gotten over that childishness?"

Mr. Herricks still could not speak. My father spoke louder, moving in his chair indignantly. "I've heard you talk about the Sermon on the Mount as if it was just another Declaration of Independence. When you pray, you speak to God politely, and remind Him that we'd like to have a little peace on this earth. You mentioned once that the parables of Jesus are excellent examples of profound human psychology. That was the Sunday when you devoted your whole lecture to the 'science of psychiatry,' and what it can do for disturbed minds." His voice became even louder and was touched with anger. "You mentioned God in passing, but there was a hell of a lot more of Freud in your lecture! Disturbed minds! You're damned right we've got disturbed minds. And why? Because our parsons think it primitive to talk about an ever-present God in the affairs of men. It never occurs to them that a human soul is thirsting for the living God, and hungering to know He is there for the asking." His voice softened and deepened. "They come to you in grief and bewilderment and pain and you quote textbooks at them, and deny them the bread of life."

"George," said my mother gently.

But Mr. Herricks lifted his head. "You are right. And I have been wrong, wickedly wrong." His eyes were stricken and ashamed. "You asked me if I believed in miracles. A week ago I might have laughed and answered that the age of miracles has passed, and that a man's strength stems from self-confidence and self-esteem. That's more psychiatry, I'm afraid." He smiled miserably. "I might have told you about adjustment to environment. I might have referred casually to God, and reminded you that the law and order of nature were miracles enough for any man. But not now. I've seen with my own eyes that the law and order of nature can be upset in a moment. I've seen that God cannot be mocked."

Edward very rarely spoke during one of my father's more strenuous arguments with anyone. He was not timid; it was just that he had the faculty of listening and absorbing. He spoke now. "I think we've come to the end. I think that God is sick of us."

"No," said my father. "It's true He is punishing us, but more than anything else I believe He is calling our attention to Him in the last hours of the world." Then he looked at me. "But Pete prayed, and the weeds were driven back. We've seen that ourselves. We've seen, these past few days, the grass growing thick and tall, and we've cut it and the cattle have eaten it without fear. What the prayer was I don't know; even Pete doesn't know. But a miracle occurred." He grinned at Johnny Carr. "And another one happened right along with it."

The news of the miracle traveled fast in our area. There was not an hour when dozens of men did not come to stand in mute wonder about our ten-yard circle of flourishing grass, and touch it, and run it reverently through their fingers. They came from Arbourville and Canton and Hillsdale; they came from as far away as a hundred miles. Some of them knelt in the grass and prayed without embarrassment. They were gaunt and frightened men, but when they saw the grass, the green and lovely grass, they smiled at each other.

Photographers and reporters came, but local news-papers did not publish a word about it. We did not tell them about my prayer, for I could not remember it.

My father had questioned me, at first quietly and reasonably, and then with frantic insistence. "Look here, Pete," he would say, "You've got to remember. Try to think, think!"

"I don't remember," I would answer despairingly. "I think I must have sat there for nearly an hour. There were a lot of prayers. I didn't have much faith they would be answered. I think I insulted God a few times. And I don't know when the weeds backed away. Perhaps it wasn't a miracle, after all. I don't know."

"It was a miracle," said my father. "There is still some-thing a man can say to God that He wants to hear. And when He hears it, perhaps He will spare us—but He wants the whole world to say it."

A month later a long black car with Government plates arrived at our house, wallowing and heaving through the weeds. My father and I went outside at the sound of voices. "Well, the news has finally got to Washington!" he said.

One of the men was our Senator, and he shook my father's hand heartily and scrutinized him. "Well, George," he said in his rich voice, "we've been hearing things about your farm."

"And I suppose it's got you all excited, Henry."

"Well, now, our state is very important to me, George. We've heard about the trouble you've been having hereabouts with these damned weeds."

My father laughed. "Just hereabouts—in this state? Henry, you wouldn't try to fool me, would you?"

"What the devil do you mean, George?" The Senator's florid face was bland, but there was fear in his eyes. "After all, I'm interested. This is my home."

"Don't get folksy, Henry. Save that for the next election, if there ever are any more elections. You know as well as I do that the weeds are all over the nation, and probably all over the world. Don't grin at me, Henry, I'm not a fool."

The Senator hastily introduced his five companions. Their names meant nothing to us, but I gathered that they were officials, and that one or two of them were botanists.

"Botanists?" My father raised his eyebrows. One of the men answered smoothly: "You've been having trouble with this—infestation. And we've heard that you've raised a patch of grass." He cleared his throat. "We want to take samples, if you'll allow us."

"Do you think you can clear away the weeds from all over the country and plant this grass instead?" My father laughed sadly. He turned to me. "This is my son, Pete. He prayed early one morning and the weeds shrank back and the grass came."

They eyed me doubtfully, as sane men eye a crank. "Well, now," said the Senator, "we all believe in prayer, don't we? Maybe Pete can give us a little demonstration. Just for the scientific records."

"You can't keep the truth from the country much

45

longer, can you?" asked my father. "Scientific records! By God! And I mean that reverently; I'm not cursing. What explanation has science for what is happening?"

One of the botanists, an older man, answered him seriously: "Frankly, it hasn't any. We refuse to admit that this isn't just a local disturbance. So would you mind taking us to that patch of grass?"

"We'll be very careful," said the younger scientist. "We won't trample on it. We need only an inch or two of it, with the earth attached."

My father looked at them thoughtfully, and then, in the hot noonday sun, we went in silence to the mysterious and leaping grass. The visitors stood about it, gazing at it thirstily. They knelt down and put their hands in it, as men put their hands in cool water. One of the botanists took notes; the other carefully cut out a section and wrapped it in a piece of chemically treated paper.

"You've fed it to your cattle?" asked the older man. "And it hasn't poisoned them?"

"They eat it as if they're starved," said my father. "I've been feeding them hay and corn, but when they smell the grass they almost go out of their minds. And there's a funny thing about it; we can cut it every day, bushels of it, but it grows like mad overnight."

Another of the men turned to me. "Could it be possible that your harrow's gasoline fumes killed the weeds?"

"That's a stupid question," my father said angrily. "Probably millions of tractors all over the country have been trying to plow them under, and they come back as fast as they're crushed and turned under the sod. Gasoline fumes!"

"Well, then," said the Senator patiently, "what explanation do you have, George?"

"It's so simple you wouldn't believe it. Pete prayed. He doesn't remember just what prayer did it, but all at once the weeds were gone and they've never come back."

The Senator put his hand on my shoulder. "Pete, how about a demonstration? Start praying again, and we'll

46

watch. I understand that the weeds shrank away in the space of a few seconds."

"Yes, pray, Pete," said my father, ironically.

"I don't remember," I answered with weariness. "Don't you think I've been trying?"

"One of these days Pete will remember. Perhaps the whole world will remember the prayer," my father said. "Until then, this will go on until we all starve and die."

The young scientist said impatiently: "There is no problem science cannot solve eventually. It's just a matter of time. Would you let us examine the machine your son used? Perhaps there is a chemical ingredient in the gasoline that killed the weeds."

They took samples of the gasoline and poured them carefully into little tubes. And then they went away, the weeds waving malignantly at the wheels of their car.

That night a new disaster struck.

Lucy, who had the only fiery temperament in the family—if one overlooked my powerful and dominant father—had hysterics suddenly, right after our meager dinner. It was rare, however, for even Lucy to lose control of herself in our disciplined household. I remember that she had just fed her younger boy his last spoonful of mashed potato and he had objected to it, and without much cause he had burst into tears. Lucy caught his little flailing arm impatiently, and when his sleeve fell back she saw a rash on his flesh. It looked, at first, like a scratch which was festering in tiny yellow dots along its length. She showed it anxiously to my mother, and when my mother tentatively touched the thing the boy squalled as if she had burned him. "He must have scratched himself some way," she said. And then she looked attentively at his small, tear-wet face and felt his forehead. "He's feverish," she added with more concern.

"The weeds!" cried Lucy desperately.

"But the children are never out," said Jean. "We watch them every moment."

Lucy lifted the boy to her lap and literally tore the clothing from him. He had half a dozen other such rashes

47

on his body. She turned very pale, and it was then that she began to weep and to scream, and her older boy burst into tears. My mother, in silence, examined the latter and mutely showed my father and the rest of us that he, too, had those strange rashes. "What is it? What's wrong?" asked Edward, fumbling his way to his wife.

My father forced the children's mouths open, and we saw that all over their tongues the tiny yellow dots of pus had broken out. "Tell me, what is it?" begged Edward, alarmed at Lucy's cries.

"The children have some sort of skin eruption," said my mother faintly. "I don't know what it is. Perhaps it's impetigo. We must call the doctor."

Suddenly Jean sprang to her feet and raced from the room. We heard her rapid footsteps on the stairs like a tattoo. I started to follow her to our baby's room, and then Lucy bent her head over her wailing children and wrung her hands, with a gesture of despairing violence. "Don't be frightened," my mother begged, trying to calm her. Perhaps it's only an allergy of some sort. Children are always getting mysterious sicknesses. Perhaps the better milk we are having now because of the grass is too rich for them. George, please don't stand there like a figure of doom and quote the Bible!" Her usually amiable voice took on a thin, high pitch. "I just can't bear it if you do that. Call the doctor!"

Edward tried to take Lucy in his arms, but she had begun to weep wildly, holding her children tightly in her arms. I saw now that the boys were definitely ill. Their eyes had a too brilliant glare under the tears, and there were white circles about their mouths.

"You are frightening the little ones," my mother implored. "Do be calm for their sake, Lucy." My father returned and announced that the doctor was on his way to our house.

Then Edward said quietly: "It can't be the weeds. I often bend down and feel them." He held out his hands for us to inspect, and turned his clouded glasses to us.

48

"You feel them—touch them?" asked my father, incredulously. "And they don't sting or poison you?"

"No. I've even handled their thorns, and I've never been pricked. Their smell is horrible, of course, but they haven't hurt me."

My father was silent, staring at my brother with deep contemplation. Jean came back into the room and relief stood out on her expressive face. She shook her head at me, and I breathed a sigh of relief.

"Of course," said my father, "they wouldn't hurt Ed."

We did not take the time to question him about this odd remark, for we had to quiet Lucy and help her take the children upstairs to their beds.

By the time the doctor arrived the two boys were tossing in a kind of delirium. Lucy was silent now; she sat in a chair near them hugging her body with both arms as if mortally cold. My father watched the examination; the doctor showed no surprise. He asked Jean to boil his hypodermic needle and he brought out a vial of streptomycin.

"You've seen this before, many times, Frank," said my father flatly. "I can tell by your face. What is it?"

The doctor hesitated. "I don't know," he said finally. "You're right; it's all over the township, and there are many cases like this in Arbourville." His eyes were tired and sunken, and he stood there brooding, looking at the children. Lucy seemed not to have heard him. "Bad?" whispered my father. Dr. Frank nodded. "Deaths?" My father's whisper was charged with dread. The doctor nodded again and his lips barely moved in answer: "Eight out of ten."

My father touched Lucy's shoulder and she started and looked up at him with blind hopelessness. "It's nothing peculiar; it's all over town, dear," he said to her. "It's a children's disease?" he asked Dr. Frank.

"Not always," he replied. But we knew he was not telling the truth. The children were being stricken down.

"Malnutrition—poor milk—canned vegetables?" faltered my mother.

"Possibly, very probably," the doctor replied, and again we knew he was lying, all but Lucy.

"They'll get better?" she begged. "It's nothing serious —please, please!"

"Of course, Lucy, they'll get better," he said, and he bent over the children with his needle. They screamed, even in their semicomatose condition. "Just keep them quiet, and as cool as possible. The heat's terrible these days, isn't it? Worst I can remember in years. Just bathe the little fellows, Lucy, with luke warm water, and dust them with this powder I'm leaving you, and when they —" again he hesitated, and his voice sank—"recover consciousness give them pieces of ice to suck. They'll come to themselves in about twenty-four hours, and then you'll have to keep them warm. They—they seem to get very cold, later."

Jean was ashen. "Is it contagious?" she asked.

The doctor shrugged. "I don't think so. It's something like pellagra, I believe—the joints and gums—"

He motioned with his head to my father and me and we followed him out into the hall. "I won't lie to you, George," said Dr. Frank. "The rash starts to bleed. When the fever drops a sort of hemorrhage which we can't control develops under the skin. Not in all cases, and let's pray it won't happen in these. For," and he looked at us dully, "the hemorrhage is a very bad symptom. The patient usually dies. The hemorrhages occur in the brain and lungs and heart, too. We've found them on autopsy."

My father had turned gray. The doctor put a hand on his shoulder. "Don't worry too much. The boys have very high fevers. The worst cases are those with subnormal or normal temperatures."

My father groaned. "What does the Health Department say?"

"It says nothing. We've already had specialists in to look at the children. George, I've been hearing about

50

your prophecies. One of them, at least, has come true. There's a plague here."

"And nowhere else?"

The doctor regarded us steadily, and we knew he was about to lie again. "Nowhere else," he said with firmness.

My father closed his eyes. "And all your wonder drugs mean nothing," he said bitterly.

Dr. Frank sighed and did not answer. He started down the stairs and we followed him. I was ill with fear for my own child. We could hear Edward and my mother trying to comfort Lucy. Jean trailed in our rear. All the light had gone out of her face, and it was strained. "Could it be smallpox?" she pleaded. "The children have been vaccinated."

"It's not smallpox," said the doctor, and now I heard his utter hopelessness. "It could be the stench of the weeds, or some kind of poison they give out. We don't know." He added: "They'll need constant care for over two weeks. You'd better tell Margaret, George, so she can relieve Lucy."

It was arranged that for safety's sake Jean was not to help Lucy and my mother. As we went up to bed together I was worried, for it was not like Jean to be so haggard and silent. She undressed without speaking and when I lay down beside her she clutched me convulsively, buried her head in my shoulder and shook with soundless sobs of despair. I stroked her fine dark hair but I had no comfort for her. My whole body ached, not only with fear but with exhaustion; each day my father and I, and our tenant farmers, buried the dead bodies of the countless birds and animals which increasingly littered the land. Whether they had died of starvation or had been poisoned we did not know. We had tried burning them, but there was no open spot now and the weeds seemed invulnerable to fire.

We had moved the baby's crib into our own room, and Jean got up several times during the night to examine the child. He slept uneasily, and he had not been gaining

51

much weight during the past months. However, there was no sign of the rash on him. When Jean returned to bed each time it was with a dry sob of weariness and fear.

She slept after midnight, but I could not. It was a moonless night, but the stars were unusually bright. I watched them and an impotent fury rushed over me. Why were we being punished, if we were indeed being punished? If there were a merciful God, why was He showing us no mercy? My faith sank away in me like the dropping of a floor. The incident of the retreat of the weeds and the growing of the grass was meaningless, accidental. I had been a superstitious fool. I thought of my father with profound contempt. This disaster which had come to the world was not supernatural; it was some natural visitation. We had only to extend our food supplies until the scientists were able to discover some method of destroying our enemy, the weeds. They were surely working on it. I thought of the dwindling, musty hay in our barns, the dwindling corn and wheat in our silos. I wondered how the cities' supplies of canned foods were holding out. The warehouses were emptying fast, too fast. We knew only of our own locality, of course, but we surmised that this was happening not only all over the country but all over the earth. And the rivers and streams were sinking again.

Only the weeds flourished. They seemed not to need water; their glistening, thorny leaves swelled with their green blood. When we had turned over some of them to permit the burying of the creatures of the fields and the woods, we saw how the thick white roots plunged deep into the ground, wet and fleshy and loathsome. Sometimes we saw our neighbors engaged in the same work of burial, but we did not hail them, nor did they hail us. We worked in silence, as if we were prisoners under guard. . . .

I lay beside Jean and clenched my fists. I thought of the scientists and shouted to them in my frantic mind: Hurry! Hurry! I could hear the ticking of the clock downstairs. Then it chimed. It was one o'clock.

As if that were a signal, the earth shivered. I felt the
bed gliding, and caught at the side of it. And then I heard
the house creaking and shifting. Jean sat up. "What was
that?" she asked faintly. Before I could answer the air
was filled with a vast sound of groaning, like subterranean
thunder. We jumped out of bed together, holding each
other, staggering a little. Then we could hear my father's
voice, and Edward's and my mother's. Edward's boys
were crying again, feebly. Catching Jean's hand I ran
to the door of our room and met the family, all except
Lucy, in the hall. Someone tried to turn on the lights,
but the switch only clicked dryly.

"An earthquake?" asked my mother, fearfully. The
starlight drifted into the hall from the end windows and
I could see my mother's nightgown and her tossed hair.

"Let's go downstairs," said my father, too quietly. "No,
Jean, don't get the baby. Here, Ed, take my arm.
Margaret, go with Pete."

The earth was still again, and the thunder had died
away. My mother found a candle and lit it. Her face
looked old and exhausted. She put the candle carefully
on a table and stood there, watching its flickering glow.

My father went to the telephone, but the line was dead.
It did not seem to surprise him. We had a battery radio
set besides one regular one. My father found it in the
kitchen and switched it on. It crackled emptily for several moments. I don't know what we expected, but we
stood about it in the shifting candlelight and waited. The
night was hot, but Jean was trembling as if she were
very cold, and I put my arm about her. Edward had
found a chair and was sitting in it, his head in his hands.

Then out of the crackling background a man's voice
spoke: "Seems there's been a slight earthquake felt here,
folks. In Arbourville some people are a little excited.
Nothing to get excited about. The telephone and electric
companies will soon have everything back in good order.
Circuits—blown fuses—well, folks, better get back to bed,
if any of you are out of bed and listening. Just a little
shake, but most of you didn't know it—"

53

"Hum," said my father.

My mother spoke, her voice thin: "I had made Lucy lie down for a while. We had a little lamp on, in the boys' room. And then it went out. I was just getting up to find another bulb when it happened."

The airless parlor was unbearably hot. "Let's go out on the porch, and be damned to the weeds," my father said. "Even though there's the stink outside at least there's a little fresh air." He paused. A great wind had come up; suddenly it battered the house and the windows rattled and the chimney moaned. We went out to the porch and the gale tore at our night clothes and rushed through our hair. We looked at the brilliant stars, hoping for clouds. The wind took away our breath, but we stood there, cooling ourselves. The cattle were lowing with sounds of distress in the barns.

Then Jean cried out and pointed at the sky. A shower of meteors illuminated the heavens, spitting and blazing like fireworks. Dumbfounded, we watched the display, which seemed endless. The earth was lit by intermittent glares, and again it groaned deep in its enormous depths. The weeds rattled all about us. Again, the earth shifted and steadied herself and the timbers of our house moaned.

We could not bear the wind and the stench and the clamor of the frightful weeds, so we went inside. We sat in the parlor, and the windows brightened and dimmed under the rain of stars. My father said: "Yet once more I shake not the earth only, but also heaven." We must have sat there for an hour, at least, before the cataract of meteors suddenly halted, and all was dark about us.

Then the lights went on, and we looked at each other and tried to smile.

We didn't learn until later that all the earth had trembled in that quake, and that in some parts of Europe there had been wide devastation and thousands of deaths. The newspapers did not speak of it. Every nation had quarantined herself.

Nor did we know then that the President had, since

April, decreed that no foreign members of the United Nations could travel beyond the confines of Manhattan Island, and that no foreign ambassador could leave the city of Washington, except by plane and on his way home.

CHAPTER SEVEN

How MANY millions of us will never forget, for as long as we live, that awful summer!

The heat did not decline. The electric fans in our houses whirred ceaselessly, for we could not open the windows. We became more and more silent and we men, working to bury the animals as fast as they died, exchanged hardly a word. Between my father and myself had risen a wall of silence, mortared with my bitter thoughts. He had stopped urging me to read the Bible to discover what it was I had prayed so long ago, for I had knocked the book from his hand when he had tried to give it to me.

The children seemed to get better, and the dreaded hemorrhages did not appear. But they cried almost constantly. Lucy and my mother grew thinner and whiter as the days and nights passed. Sometimes I would see their faces at the bedroom windows as I came from the barns. They would look out over the savage ocean of weeds and at the terrible cloudless sky and at the matted hills. The food on our plates became more meager daily. When my father went into Arbourville for flour and salt and sugar and coffee he would bring back only half as much as we needed. The telephone never rang at all; we were hedged in from our fellow men by our universal despair.

Invariably we asked my father for news from town. So far, he related, only the gardens and lawns were overrun with the weeds, and the people, though obviously frightened, appeared to believe that it was "only a local manifestation," and that the "drought" was responsible for the sudden decline in available meats and milk and sugar and flour. They were restive and sullen and talked angrily about the Government. My father called on young Mr. Herricks several times, though we no longer could attend church. He did not tell us then that Mr. Herricks had informed him, with grief, that so many children were dying that he was constantly attending funerals.

The farm journals remained bland, filled with discussions of new fertilizers, the possibility of "floors" under the price of cattle, criticisms of the Department of Agriculture, lively editorials, "women's interests," a humorous comment or two about "the trouble some of our farmers are having with a thistle-like weed in the fields—pesky devils!"

My father never missed watching a television session of the United Nations in action, even if he had to come sweating in from the infested fields for that purpose. He would sit, smoking his pipe, his eyes fixed on the screen. Very often I joined him. "Look at them," he would mutter, pointing with his pipe stem. "Look at their faces. They're haunted, every damn one of them. Look how they glance sideways at each other, wanting to know if other nations are dying as they are dying."

Usually they talked aimlessly, and sometimes there would be a strange, halting silence in the midst of a discussion.

One day the head of the American delegation rose to announce that the President was hoping to reduce the arms budget even more during the next session of

Congress, and that he was sending a message to the Communist members of the United Nations urging that they, in all sincerity, give assurance that they planned no new aggressions or conspiracies in any part of the world. This had been the signal, in the past, for the Russian delegates to display belligerence and to begin to belabor "the West" for its "imperialistic designs on the Peoples Democracies." But on this day the Russians sat for a few long moments in their chairs, staring emptily before them. At last their leader stood up and in a mild and slightly trembling voice declared that Russia too sought only peace.

"Look at that Russian fellow," my father said. "Remember how he was always shouting and accusing and glaring and waving his arms? He's looking mighty sober these days, almost human. He doesn't even sit studying his watch when someone else is speaking, the way he used to do. I wonder what he's thinking? He looks scared half to death, and the others do, too."

My father stopped watching the sessions for a while when his oldest grandson suddenly died, and we were plunged into a time of grief. The child's body was, over-night, stained with dark purple patches. We had to wait five days for a grave for him.

Lucy and Edward were inconsolable. It was bad enough to see Lucy's white, dry face. It was infinitely more crushing to see Edward's tears seeping down from his blind eyes. For some strange reason Edward's tears aroused in me an incomprehensible guilt. There was no obvious reason for that guilt that I could discover. I had always loved and protected him; I loved his children as if they had been my own. Yet when I saw his tears something unbearably remorseful stabbed at my heart. Once I was on the verge of crying out to him: "Forgive me!" I caught back the words just in time. For what should he forgive me? I must, I thought, be going out of my mind. I was not the cause of his child's death.

No one came to see us after the anguished funeral.

We sat alone, hardly able to talk. Lucy tended the younger child and would not leave him for a moment. With immense gratitude we knew that he was recovering. But it was piteous to hear him call for his brother.

The September sun was wrathful, and though the trees were slowly turning to old yellow and there was a hint of crimson among the leaves of the maples, the heat mounted. No rain had fallen anywhere in the world for almost two months. Once we read a scientific account of the retreat of the polar caps. "This will enable more and more land to be cultivated for food," exclaimed one farm journal delightedly. Food? There would never be food again, I thought; I knew that my father was right.

It was October—a burning, relentless October—when Johnny Carr came to see us with his wife, a worn and quiet woman. They came in a wallowing tractor, for no other sort of vehicle could move over the land. Johnny, not much more than fifty, seemed a decade older. "I just heard," he said, as he shook my father's hand, "that Ed's boy died. Got it in a roundabout way. You didn't know that my oldest boy's little girl died, too, out in Missouri where he'd bought his own farm. All the kids are dying, everywhere."

My father, after expressing his regret for Johnny's own grief, turned to my mother and said gently: "You see, Margaret, it wasn't that our neighbors and friends didn't care about us. They didn't know; it's all being kept from them."

Johnny had always been a sure source of news of our community. He told us of the many young deaths in the township and all over the country. "And there's another thing," he said. "Another kind of disease, hitting men and women. Like dysentery. No wonder, with no fresh food anywhere. Deaths? Sure, thousands of them. I hear from my friends about it. Maybe it's right here around us, too." He patted his stomach uneasily. "Sometimes I think I've got appendicitis, it hurts so bad."

"Don't go imagining things, Johnny Carr," said his wife. She began to cry. "I never saw Jim's little girl, though we'd planned to go out there this summer." My mother went to her and they wept together. Lucy sat apart, stony, rigid, staring straight before her. She would not permit even Edward to touch her.

"Pete, you remember that prayer yet?" asked Johnny. He looked ill and very tired.

I replied angrily: "For God's sake, don't talk about it! There wasn't any prayer. It just happened. Maybe my machine did it, after all. Why doesn't the damn Government call out all the bulldozers all over the country and put the Army in charge of them to plow up the weeds?"

"Didn't you know?" said Johnny, his rough voice almost pitying. "The Government's been doing just that, Pete, and it's no use. They come back faster than ever. They've been trying everything—fire, weed-killers, gasoline. You'll never read about it in the papers, but the Government isn't sitting on its—" He glanced at the women and continued—"rear end. A couple of fellows I know in Texas and another in Kansas tell me the scientists are working night and day. Now they're scared. They did some things and the weeds went back a little, but then in a day or two there they were again, thicker and stronger. In some places they reach to the second floors of houses. Funny, they don't strangle the trees, but they kill off everything else."

My father nodded. "Are you boiling the water for yourselves and your stock as the papers advised us to?"

"No, George. Never boiled water in my life. No typhoid around here; never has been. A lot of—" again he caught himself—"foolishness." He put his hand to his stomach again and winced. "Incidentally, there's no fruit coming out of Florida, no oranges, lemons or anything. And the cattle there are dying off as fast as they are here."

Mrs. Carr had brought with her a big basket of home-canned fruit and vegetables for the children. "I got a whole cellar full, enough for a couple of years for us. Margaret, you just call me when you want more. I've got tomatoes here, and beans and corn and peas and fruit, and my own tomato juice."

We, like Johnny, had slaughtered many of our lean pigs ahead of time and had smoked them.. We had killed off much of our remaining cattle and had stored the meat in our huge freezers before the cattle could die.

"Shouldn't wonder if the Government started asking around among the farmers how much food they got on hand for themselves," said Johnny with a weak grin. "Did the Grange fellows come snooping around here a couple of weeks ago like they did with us? Oh, it was all smooth; they said they were just making a survey to see if the farm women were putting up canned goods like they used to, or were they depending on the stores for commercial goods. What goods? They know as well as we do that there aren't any."

My father and I knew all about the Grange agents, for they had been at our house, too. "The stocks in the cities must be getting dangerously low," my father said. "I shouldn't be surprised if very soon the Government issues orders against hoarding and tries to confiscate as much food as possible from the farmers to feed the town people. For if the cities get out of hand—"

They did, but that was later.

After Johnny and his wife had left we went to the barns and met our tenant farmers there. One of them had obviously been crying; he was a silent young man as a rule, and even when my father prodded him for an explanation it was some time before he confessed that he had, that very morning, buried two of his children. "Mr. George," he asked in despair, "what in hell is happening to us?"

I was afraid my father would begin one of his jeremiads, and I tensed myself for enraged rebuttal, but he only said, with compassion: "I don't know, son."

I turned away from him in the barns and went to console our last young bull, who always greeted me with searching and pleading eyes. I had almost reached him when he threw up his head, glared at me, tossed his horns

61

and uttered what was almost a scream. He threshed in his stall, rolling his eyes madly, trying to tear himself loose. "Boy, boy," I said, alarmed. "I'm not going to hurt you." My father and our tenants came up quickly. I tried to pat the poor beast and he glared at me again with frenzy. "He's never acted this way before," I began. But one of the men shouted and started back, pointing. A loathsome creature about ten inches long, resembling a scorpion, was scuttling away in the straw of the stall. The bull's ankles were bleeding.

My father, who was a man of great courage, acted quickly. He seized a pitchfork and routed out this new horror. It was a dark red color, and it was not a scorpion. With paralyzed fascination we watched it as it fought against the prongs of the pitchfork. We had never seen such a creature before. It lashed with a dozen venomous legs; it stared up at us with tiny black eyes. From its elongated mouth there dripped blood and poison. My father stabbed at it repeatedly; it died very hard and very slowly, its armored body writhing.

The bull was sinking to his knees now, rolling in a death agony, and the other cattle began threshing in their stalls. My father rushed about the barn, whipping aside straw, plunging his pitchfork in every direction. He killed three more of the monstrous things, stamping, thrusting. And we just stood there, appalled.

My father, gasping and panting, swung to us. "What's the matter with you imbeciles?" he shouted. "Get more forks. Go all through the barns! Hurry!"

We recovered ourselves, trembling. We picked up forks and hammers and heavy wrenches. We went through every building including that which housed our dwindled flocks of chickens. We killed ten of the creatures in the next hour. We were covered with sweat and shaking with dread when we finally gathered together again. "Not scorpions," said my father in a hushed voice. "I don't know what they are. Watch yourselves when you walk through the weeds. They must be full of them."

We had been keeping the barn doors ajar so that our

animals could have some air. Now we shut them tightly. In absolute hopelessness we parted. I followed my father into the house fighting waves of nausea. My father, who was ashen, calmly went through all the rooms, examining every corner, the ceilings, moving furniture to peer behind it, sharply shutting any slightly opened window, lifting the edges of rugs, and shaking curtains. My mother trailed him asking anxious questions. But he did not answer her until he had toured the house and satisfied himself. Then he turned to my mother and took her in his arms. "Margaret, there's something else. Our last bull just died; he was bitten by something like a scorpion. Don't cry, this is too important. You and the girls must never put your bare feet down on the floors. You must never go to bed without examining everything in the room. Keep looking in the clothes at least twice a day. Our lives depend upon it. This is no time to panic."

But my mother was already in a panic. I called for Jean and she came down. She listened to my explanation, her dark eyes widening with fear. But she merely nodded at me, without speaking, and tried to comfort my mother while my father went to the telephone and called the Grange offices. And then he was yelling into the mouthpiece: "Don't sound so damned incredulous! If they're here, right on our farm, they're all over and you know it! Don't you think it's about time we admitted to each other what's happening everywhere? What's this infernal conspiracy of silence? D'you think it's going to keep us and our stock alive?"

He listened, panting savagely. And then he laughed loudly and bitterly. "Panic? What of it? Is it better for us all to die? Oh, you've been getting reports, have you? Nothing to be alarmed about, is it? Put poison around? That's nice, that's very nice, Bill. And what about our stock eating the poison, too? Oh, you've thought of that! Keep them tied up? You're a wonderful help. Where's Lester?" There was a silence. Father repeated, in a slower voice: "In Washington. So Grange presidents

63

are in Washington. And what good will that do?" He slammed down the receiver.

He turned to me and said: "Pete, we're fighting for our lives now. We're up against more than the prospects of starvation sometime in the future. There's death all around us." He put his hand on my shoulder, and there were tears in his eyes. "Pete, Pete," he said. "You've been avoiding me; you've begun almost to hate me. That's because you're frightened, I know. But we've got to stand together now."

My mother was crying violently, and the sound of her anguish brought even Lucy down the stairs. When Jean, as quietly as possible, explained, Lucy screamed loudly just once and then flew up the stairs to her boy's room. We could hear her running about, opening closet doors, banging them shut, wrenching draperies across windows. She had been shaken out of her apathy of sorrow, and we listened to her as she prepared again to fight for her son's life. We heard the boy sobbing in his bed, and then her soothing voice as she gathered him to her.

My father sighed. "Poor girl, poor girl," he murmured. He smiled at Jean, who had succeeded in calming my mother a little. "How's your boy, Jean? Better keep him in his crib every minute, and never let him stand on the floor even though he's begun to walk." He fanned himself with his damp handkerchief.

His voice was like a strength in the hot room, and I forgot all my antagonism for him. Then I remembered Edward. Where was he? My father and I stared at each other in consternation. We had forgotten him in our terror, or he had not been in any of the buildings. We jostled each other as we ran to the door, and rushed out on to the porch. Edward was walking slowly through the weeds, feeling his way with his cane. His head was bent and the implacable sun was gleaming on his glasses. I wanted to call to him to hurry, and even took a step towards him, but my father held me back. It wasn't until Edward mounted the porch steps that my father took his arm.

My brother listened to what my father told him, shaking his head in mute disbelief. Then he said: "You must be right, Dad. I heard things rustling in the weeds. But they were rustling away from me. I thought they were mice or rabbits."

My father was very still. "They rustled away from you, Ed?"

He nodded. "When I think of it it seems to me that they were trying to get away from me, and not to get near me. They—clattered. I thought it was a funny sound at the time." He started. "Where's Lucy?" He walked with the rapidity and sureness of a seeing man into the house, calling for his wife.

My father and I stood and looked at each other. "Could it be," he asked at last, "that the thorns don't prick Ed, or tear at him, and the—things—run away from him because God is merciful and knows that he has suffered enough, and isn't guilty of anything?"

I wanted to scoff, and then I couldn't speak. Something was stirring in my mind, something which seemed of the most urgent importance. Not guilty of anything? It was a clue to something I desperately needed to remember. "What is it, Pete?" asked Father softly. But I could only shake my head.

My father went to the telephone again, and, begging my mother to stop crying, called Johnny Carr's house. There was no answer for a long time, and then finally Mrs. Carr answered, choking with tears. Johnny had died only an hour before, suddenly, in a kind of collapse, after complaining all morning of his stomach. My father sat down and covered his face with his hands.

CHAPTER EIGHT

In the days that followed, the impossible days, we found more than a score of the new and living plague, but not before they had killed most of our livestock. Life had been hard enough before; now it was intolerable. My father took to calling his farmer friends, who were frantic. Their wives or sons or parents were ill with the mysterious dysentery, their children were dying, their cattle were being killed, their chickens were found dead every morning. Now it was out in the open, the whole nightmare, and no longer a secret kept by one man from another. We all besieged our local newspapers to publish the facts. The editors said quietly: "We can't. We've got our orders."

We tried poison bait. The bait disappeared, and there were no signs of any corpses. We hunted out the creatures at least twice a day, and crushed or stabbed them to death after incredible effort. Once my father found one in his own bedroom; he killed it, and showed it to me without speaking. We did not tell my mother and the girls.

In the meantime, though it was full October, the heat did not slacken. In fact, it became worse. We should have had frost by now.

Our work was so prodigious these days that it was some time before we became fully aware of what we had been subconsciously seeing for many days. The sky, during the day, was an unchanging, brassy yellow, in which the sun shone murkily. And a new stench was added to that of the weeds; a curious odor like sulphur. We began to cough in it. The night did not dissipate it. When the moon shone its disk was large and golden, and seemed very close to the earth.

I began to feel myself giving up in spite of my efforts. I began to join my father in the sitting room, and I took the Bible from him silently and read verses to which he pointed. "The abomination of desolation" was on us. Even I became convinced, as the days passed, that our earth was destroying us upon a command, that she received our bodies reluctantly, that she gave her air to us grudingly and with hatred.

My father's fatal calm returned to him. He would watch the meetings of the United Nations and he would make no comment. I saw the faces of the delegates growing more and more haggard every day, their voices more and more dull and abstracted. Then one day a Russian delegate rose to his feet and in a diminished tone without triumph announced that his country had developed a bomb far superior to the hydrogen bomb, "capable of destroying a huge city with one blow." The other delegates listened, listlessly. They made no reply. The Russian looked at them imploringly, and they looked back at him, their shoulders sagging. The Russian sat down. Now he covered his eyes with his hand, and the television commentator announced that the session was closing early that day. We saw papers and briefcases being lifted; we saw seeking and desperate eyes. The delegates moved slowly away from their tables, not exchanging a single word. The picture faded.

The first of November came and brought no relief. I

think we had all been waiting for frost, in the faint hope that it would kill off the weeds. But they flourished more energetically. They were heaped about the house; they had invaded our porch. Now they mounted like ivy over the walls of the house and thrust their tendrils at the sills of our upper windows. We dared not attempt to cut them away. When the moon shone it was as if snakes waved beyond the glass, searching for us.

Our food supplies sank steadily. There was no longer any milk for the children. We adults ate moldy potatoes and smoked or frozen meat. There were still the canned vegetables and fruits for the children, but they, too, were dwindling dangerously. There was no more coffee or sugar or flour in the stores, and butter was becoming scarce. My father found an old grinding mill in one of our barns and my mother and the girls ground up corn for bread for us. Our wheat was gone.

Now our local Grange issued a plea to those farmers who had a plentiful supply of canned goods from the past summer to share it with their neighbors who had children. The women looked over their supplies and filled baskets for the children, and tractors picked them up and distributed them. So long as a child remained alive we were prepared to try to save it. However, the children continued to die throughout the township. Schools and colleges did not reopen throughout the country and we no longer went to town.

The radio spoke of the "countrywide" heat. It would be good for the late crops. This was a blessing, said the gaunt-faced commentators, because the season had been late in starting. "Farmers are confident," said one of the young men, and he gazed out of the screen with haunted eyes.

"It's coming close now," said my father. We did not ask for an explanation.

The United Nations called an indefinite recess. "So they've all been summoned home," said my father with renewed grimness. On the day that the recess was called a Dutch delegate rose, leaned on the table, and slowly looked about him. He began to plead, in an exhausted voice, for the ancient dream of a united Europe. "Not for wars, but for peace," he said. "Not for aggression, but for cooperation." The delegates rubbed their chins absently, and moved restlessly in their seats. "If we don't cooperate, we shall die," said the Hollander wearily. The delegates refused to meet each other's eyes. Our farm journals did not arrive for the month of November, and our daily newspapers were issued only twice a week. They carried very few death notices.

And the yellow skies became more sulphurous and the plague of venomous creatures increased in the weeds, and the heat intensified, and there were "earthquakes in divers places." Sometimes we would awaken to the trembling of the earth, and more often showers of meteors flared through our night skies.

On the day before Thanksgiving, on a particularly hot day, my mother suddenly sickened and had to be carried to her bed.

We knew then the most complete despair. She had been our gentle hope and our confidence, soothing our fears with silent smiles and eyes full of love. We sat about in the house, in the reflection of the fearful yellow light at our windows, and we could not speak. If mother died, then we would indeed give up.

Lucy and Jean sat with her constantly, their children in their arms. Mother became delirious, our doctor did not reply to our frenzied calls. We pleaded with other doctors to come, but they could take no more patients. Besides, they assured us, nothing could be done; only careful nursing held out any hope for those stricken. We did not find our until much later that our own doctor had died on the day my mother became ill.

But my mother did not die. After two weeks of tortured illness she began to mend. My father, that night, knelt down among us and offered up his thanks to God, and one by one we knelt with him.

We who lived in the country did not know that the

first food riots broke out in the cities in early December.

The small towns, situated, as Arbourville is situated, in the middle of a rural township, did not riot until much later than the cities, for they knew that the farmers could not farm and that their existence was tied up with our own. Their lavish suburban lawns were overgrown with weeds, and they had no gardens now, and they understood that the farms had no vegetable gardens either. Moreover, they were closer to us, had relatives and friends among us, and knew of our daily struggle to survive.

My father had taken, recently, to buying a newspaper again. Our mail deliveries had sunk to almost nothing now, and my father had to wait for his newspapers until the local post office could send out its mailmen on borrowed tractors. Upon receiving them, he read them thoroughly. Out of curiosity, I read them too, automatically noticing that "food supplies, because of the nation-wide drought, are not in the best of supply; fruit and vegetables not of the best quality nor plentiful." The packing companies were "seriously concerned about the shortage of vegetables and fruit for commercial canning." We would not this year, be able to ship "our usual large quota of wheat to nations suffering from famine." However, the papers concluded optimistically, the "good weather, the prolonged growing season" would certainly result in excellent crops next year.

It is doubtful if one city man in a million had read even these slight straws blowing in the wind of disaster. He was probably more interested in the announcement of the Government that "scientists had succeeded in cultivating superior vegetables in water by scientifically controlled administration of necessary chemicals." The man in the city did not know that the few vegetables he saw in his markets these days resulted from such artificial cultivation.

It was about the first or second day of December that my father suddenly exclaimed: "Well, here it is, at last!" He read to us an editorial dated nearly ten days before.

"We are at a loss to understand the apparent hoarding or withholding by the farmer of his products from the city markets. There can be no other explanation for the current shortage in our cities, and for the high prices demanded for such necessities as meat and milk and flour. True, there has been a wide drought in various areas of the country, but surely not serious enough to account for the slender supplies on the shelves of our shops. The Administration should immediately take steps to show the farmer that he is demanding prices beyond the ability of the average man to pay; that he is pricing himself out of the market and will ultimately be the loser. The Administration should enforce immediate application of emergency laws to force the farmer . . . hoarding—"

My father threw aside the paper and stared at us somberly. "Well, there it is," he said. "We're hoarding." He stood up and stamped around the room. "Why doesn't the Government give the facts of life to the cities? Are they afraid they'll riot?"

They were already rioting, not in full panic as yet, but in isolated instances. Mobs were angrily overthrowing market stalls filled with the artificially cultivated vegetables, threatening the owners of shops, furiously demanding milk for their children, and carrying off armloads of the canned meats and fruits and defiantly resisting the pleas of shopkeepers to "ration" themselves.

But this the newspapers did not report, on orders from Washington. They only began to berate the farmer for his selfishness, some in measured tones, some in raucous headlines. We did not know of these unorganized riots for some time. We had some slight suspicion when the Farm Bureau sent us an apologetic but alarming leaflet. "The President has issued an emergency act because of the drought, and the Army has been commissioned to inspect the farmers' private stocks of meats and other foods. We ask our members to cooperate completely."

"So they're going to take our food," said Father bitterly. He held the leaflet in his hand. "And if we die," he continued, "who, then, if the earth ever yields again,

71

will produce the food to save the world?" He threw the leaflet on the table. "The Army," he muttered. "It must be even worse than I thought. The Army!"

The Army, represented by two khaki-colored bull-dozers filled with boys in uniform, arrived three days later. We heard their amazed shouts, their curses, their wonder at the devouring weeds long before we saw them. We went out onto the porch, this ominously warm day in December, and watched the bulldozers skidding and slipping toward us through the rank undergrowth. "What the hell's wrong here?" yelled one soldier, look-ing down with horror. "Raisin' these things for some-thin'?"

My father just stood there, his big legs solidly planted on the ripples of weeds on the porch, smoking in silence. My mother and the girls looked out fearfully from the door, but Edward and I flanked my father.

"It's all over the damn country," said another soldier. They peered at us, empty-faced and bewildered. The yellow sky loomed behind the bulldozers, lending an eerie ochre tint to the huge-thorned leaves of the weeds and to the soldiers' faces. The smoke from their cigarettes rose idly in the still and poisoned air.

Then a young officer, brisker and older than the others, prepared to get down from the bulldozer. My father called to him sharply: "Haven't they told you yet? The thorns on these things will pierce through your clothing, and there are creatures like scorpions hidden in them which can kill you with one sting. If you must get down, all of you, pull those machines closer to the porch where the weeds aren't so thick, and step carefully."

The officer shrank back, after one incredulous stare at my father. Then he gave a muttered order and one bull-dozer wheeled and grunted to the steps of the porch. The officer gingerly stepped down, and my father grasped his arm and pulled him to the shallowest place. "Come into the house. We've still got some cider, and you look as if you need it." The boy made the door in one long

72

leap, and then in our parlor he said, panting a little: "Damnedest thing I ever saw! Is it all over here?"

"It's all over the world," said my father, quietly.

"I don't believe it!"

"You will, son, you will. Why don't you sit down?"

The officer sat down. He fumbled for a cigarette, and he seemed very sober. "We were sent by train from Camp Upton last night, and the bulldozers were shipped with us. We didn't know why. We were told to interview every farmer in this area and see what he's got—hoarded." He tried to smile at us, then produced a notebook and pencil.

"Any of these weeds at Camp Upton?" asked my father with interest.

"Well, sir, there must have been. The camp's all concrete and steel, and we wondered for a long time why we were confined to the grounds. I didn't see any of these—things—until we got to Arbourville this morning. And you're the first farmer we've found at home. Every other place was deserted." He frowned. "Where are the rest of them?"

My father sat on the edge of his chair and leaned toward the boy. "They were probably out burying their dead. Haven't you heard about the dysentery yet, and the dying children? Or have they kept this from you, too?"

Very slowly the boy paled. "You mean there's an epidemic? I thought so! You keep missing some of the fellows at camp. We thought it was flu, or something. And I haven't heard from home for over a week. Maybe someone there is sick—"

My father did not comment. The officer's hand was trembling, though he attempted to appear efficient. "Look, sir, let's make it brief and honest. What meat do you have stored, how much in the way of vegetables and corn and canned goods?"

My mother, who was sitting at a distance, started to her feet, tears in her eyes. "We have almost nothing to live on ourselves. We're eating old potatoes and dried-out

73

apples from last year, and canned milk we bought a few months ago. I'm saving my own canned goods for the children—we have two of them here, just babies. And we slaughtered almost all our pigs and the bigger part of the cattle which hadn't been killed already."

The boy sat there and looked at her. He kept moistening his lips for a long time, his eyes roving from face to face. He whispered finally: "Is it that way with all the farmers?" My father nodded. The boy stared for another long moment. Then he cried: "It can't be! They told us you were all hoarding your goods for higher prices, and that you'd have to be forced to give them up!"

"I know," my father said. "I've been reading the newspapers, too." He glanced at the officer's shoes. "I suppose you'll want to investigate for yourself. Pete, find a pair of high boots this kid can wear. We don't want another death on our hands."

I brought a pair of boots, and the soldier put them on, his hands shaking. My father and I led him outside, through the rear door facing the barns.

My father stepped down and the officer followed nervously. I brought up the rear. The boy was terrified of the weeds; they crunched under his boots; they lifted their tentacles and snatched at his clothing. He shrank, when he heard the vile scuttling in the depths. "Keep your hands high," warned my father. "Shoulder-high." He led the way, probing into the nauseous thickets with the pitchfork he always carried. By the time we reached our almost empty barns the officer's face was sick and pale with fear.

He looked about the shadowy reaches of the barn. "Four cows, three hogs, about fifty chickens," he wrote down in his book. He inspected the fruit bins, and my father lighted a lantern so that he could see the little mounds of shriveled apples and pears, the few bags of our remaining potatoes. He wrote down what he had found, his hands trembling more and more. My father showed him the silos. "Enough to feed the stock for

74

about four months more," he said. He opened the freezers. "Meat for us and the children for about five months, if we're careful. Want to look down in our cellar and inspect our canned goods, too?"

He did. He went up and down the rows of my mother's preserves, and what Mrs. Carr had given us. "Seems a lot," he said with relief. "Fifty cans of tomatoes; sixty-five cans of peaches; forty cans of pears; seventy of corn and peas and beans, and one hundred cans of milk! Why a city family could live on all this for a year or more!"

"And when that's gone?" prodded my father.

The boy grinned. "Why, you'll have another big crop, won't you?"

It was useless. He became very brisk now. "Sorry, but there'll be a truck along in about three days and you'll have to give up half of what you've got. Orders. You'd better set a fair market price on it, and you'll get a check from Washington, eventually."

We were back in the parlor again. The officer started to take off the borrowed boots, but my father said: "No. Keep them; you'll need them. And maybe you won't find other farmers as co-operative as we are. They might just let you go out into the weeds and among the poisonous things. You see, when a man has a family to feed and he's threatened with starvation, he gets angry."

The boy was grateful. He became very serious. "In emergencies we all have to share with each other. You learn that in the Army. And we're a Christian people, aren't we?"

"No," said my father compassionately. "What gave you that idea?"

He went outside with the young man, who seemed to be thinking very deeply. Father waved as the bulldozers lumbered off in the awful yellow light.

The huge pickup truck came the next day, wallowing and swaying through the weeds. It took away half of our food. My father did not protest or interfere, nor did our immediate neighbors, though they were enraged and wild with fear. We did not hear, for a long time, that thousands of farmers in other parts of the country had wrecked the trucks and attacked the drivers. In many places the National Guard and the Army were called out to enforce the new law and to subdue the desperate farmers. The cities had one small last reprieve.

CHAPTER NINE

IN OUR TOWNSHIP there had always been the usual number of enemies and friends, just as in every other community, but during these past months the enmity had slowly decreased in the face of the universal threat of death. The last hostility between any farmer and his neighbor disappeared entirely in December. What children still lived had to be saved, to make the earth fruitful again; the farmer, the sower, had to be saved, too, to plant crops and breed cattle and pigs and chickens and beget children. We operated by instinct; we had to preserve each other. There was something atavistic in the way we all took stock of our remaining food, something mysteriously dedicated. We got out our tractors, all of us, lumbered through the weeds to the highways, and met at the Grange Hall. We reported what canned goods and meats we had left and we reported the number of children in our families and the number of those young adults who could be expected to marry and produce children. And then we apportioned the food among ourselves—so much canned milk for so many babies, so much meat for vigorous young adults, so much corn, so much wheat and flour. The feed for the stock was apportioned, too. The cows had to be fed, the bulls preserved. No man was coerced; it was not necessary to appeal even to those who in the past had been noted for their greed. The law of life was more important in these terrible days than the security of an individual.

It was my father, rather than our wasted president, who managed the whole affair—my father who stood like an oak among that large assembly of farmers and justly divided what we all had for common survival. The stocks were so low that no child over eighteen months was to be permitted any canned milk; no adult over fifty was to be permitted more than one pound of meat a week. A large room in the Grange was set aside for the reception of the goods, and two armed guards were to be constantly on watch.

Our president, Lester Hartwick, expressed some alarm over this arrangement. He lived in Arbourville, though he had a large farm operated by tenant farmers, and he was aware of the temper of the town, and of the other towns in the vicinity. "I don't know, George," he said, in his newly feeble voice. "I've seen something recently, something I don't like. There are strangers, young men and women, in town. City people, from the looks of them. They look hungry, like they were being eaten up inside, and they scuttle around asking questions. I thought at first they were Government agents, but they're not. I hear they meet almost every night, each time in a different place. The Wittmer Hotel swarms with them."

He shook his head. "They're here for no good purpose. I've seen them get into conversations with the town people, and I've heard them talk about 'greedy, hoarding farmers,' and why don't the farmers share all their stored goods, and why don't the town folks do something about it. The farmer knows that the Government's already confiscated half his supplies, and sometimes more, but the town people don't know it. I've tried to tell them, at our Elks Meeting—and they've laughed

78

at me. It's ugly, I tell you. And that's why I'm afraid of keeping the food in the Grange hall. Sure we can bring it in at night, but I tell you these strangers have eyes in the backs of their heads. One of them'd see us."

My father considered this, rubbing his chin thoughtfully. "That's true," he said. "But we have to have a point of distribution. And even if we picked out some remote barn they'd find out. Arbourville is the logical center, so we'll have to take a chance. We'll have to keep a watch, all the time."

The best guns were selected for the guards, who were all young veterans and sharpshooters. "Remember," said my father with some sadness, "that you aren't to shoot at sight, or even threaten to shoot. You are to shoot, and then only to wound, if our food is attacked. If they see we are determined to protect ourselves perhaps they won't try anything."

We brought in our trucks at night. And each truck, as we rolled into Arbourville, was guarded by keen-eyed young men who held their guns ready, hoping they would not have to use them. We came—sweltering in the heat, though this was the middle of December—under hot moons and brittle stars. And we stored the canned goods neatly, prepared our rationing papers, and put the meat into freezers donated for that purpose. The streets were empty, for we usually arrived around midnight, yet I had the eerie sense that we were watched from behind dark windows and from shadowy corners. It was impossible to keep the operation secret, and we knew it.

Government rationing was already established in town and city stores, and the people there were eating much better than the farmers. But they, too, were hungry, if not as hungry as we. We could feel their wrath like a fog in the air. We could feel their panic, their blind determination to survive.

We heard, later, that every farming community had done just what we had done.

79

No newspaper reported what the Grangers had arranged so that the cultivators of the earth could live. But their silence, their merciful silence, was not to help us in the long run. What the newspapers did not print the people discovered, through their enemies, and ours. They did not understand until almost the last that in assuring our own survival we were attempting to assure theirs, too. Only our mutual enemies knew it, and they were plotting that as few of us as possible should live.

The city newspapers reported that turkeys were in "short supply" this year, and that few of them would appear in the markets for Christmas. "But, under rationing, there will be ample meat and pork, if the people are careful and do not resort to black markets."

"Black markets!" exclaimed my father, appalled. "Is it possible that our confiscated food is actually finding its way, in the cities, to black markets? Haven't the people yet learned that money is without value now?"

On the twentieth of December I took my turn, with my friend Sam Mosler, at guarding the food in Arbourville. My father decided to accompany me. We parked our tractor on a side street, and walked, our footsteps ringing, through the dark empty town. Above our heads the jaundiced moon rolled without shedding any light, and we could not bear to look at it. But we were thankful that the sulphurous air was a little less warm than usual. And here in town, at least the stench of the weeds was not quite so pronounced. The bleak faces of the houses and shops were not engulfed in a green and deathly tide, as our own homes and barns were.

We reached the locked doors of the Grange and gave the signal for the day. The great doors were opened cautiously, and we saw the young guards we were to relieve, their fingers tight on their guns. The doors closed behind us. My father inspected the stocks of canned goods and meat, and shook his head in silence. They were dangerously low. While Sam and I talked, my father went over the rationing papers. Some had been cancelled; too many had been cancelled. The children were still dying, and so were their parents. When a farm family dwindled the survivors immediately cancelled their papers, and sent back goods previously taken under voluntary rationing. The food of the dead was keeping our stocks from running out too soon.

My father rustled the papers with sorrow, sometimes exclaiming aloud in grief. He sat under the shallow light overhead, his hair almost white now, his big frame emaciated, his strong face gaunt. Yet he still exuded strength and calm power. Sam and I moved about with our guns, listening intently at the doors, pausing for a moment or two beside barred and shuttered windows. We were restless; we were hungry and very tired. We perched, at two o'clock in the morning, on the long table which held the papers, and we ate our meager sandwiches and shared a withered apple, and drank a little whisky. We checked our guns and our ammunition, and leafed through magazines and newspapers, yawning, stretching, waiting for the yellow dawn when we would be relieved.

Sam was a little, wiry fellow, full of funny stories, and a wonderful mimic. He entertained us with considerable animation, and soon he had my father and me laughing.

But by three o'clock I was numb with fatigue. Sam's stories began to lag, and even he would break off and stare before him with strange, fixed eyes. We were both again sitting on the edge of the table when we heard a sound outside. We sprang to our feet, seizing our guns. The sound was repeated, and we knew it was a peremptory knock. This was immediately followed by a hoarse shout set up by many voices. "Let us in! Damn you, let us in! We want the food! Give us the food, you damned, greedy farmers!"

My father caught me back, and he was as gray as old ash. "They may be armed," he muttered. "Wait, let me talk to them." He went to the door and called through it: "Who are you? Any Arbourville men there?"

There was a silence, followed by a vague muttering. Then a man replied in a voice none of us recognized:

81

"Yes, ten of them. And we all want the food." It was a strange voice, hard and metallic.

"I don't know you," said my father. "But I think I know what you are. If any of our own people are there, let them speak."

There was a short pause. Sam and I flanked my father, our hands firm on our guns. Then another voice spoke, rough and almost sheepish: "You there, George? This is Joe Schultz. You know, I got that market on High Street. My market's almost empty. The town people got to live, too, you know that, George. You farmers have lots of food hidden away. We got a right to this, and you better let us take it." Another familiar voice echoed: "We don't want no trouble, George. I've got five kids, and the ration isn't enough. Let us in."

My father said: "Look here, boys, if we had food at home would we be storing some it here for the other farmers? And if we had food why should we put it here? Be sensible, boys. Stop and think. We had half our food taken away from us by the Government early this month, and now it's on your shelves, what there was of it, and you're eating better than we are—"

The metallic voice interrupted him harshly: "Lies, lies! The farmers have always exploited labor and the masses in the cities. They believe in the material welfare of the greedy few."

"I've heard that song and dance before," said my father, "and so have a lot of you boys out there. 'The material welfare of the greedy few,' the man says. And who are they? Men like him. Not you fellows with shops, and your friends and neighbors, people trying to earn a decent living. Boys, go home, and before you go run these rascals out of town. They're the enemies of all of us."

Still another familiar voice said uncertainly: "I know old George; he never told nobody a lie in his life."

"Your friend is lying now, Mr. Baldwin. Honest, peaceful men don't hoard food needed by the desperate, and arm themselves to guard it from their neighbors."

"George is no liar!" shouted Joe Schultz. "The man that says he is is going to get his teeth pounded down his throat!"

"Good," muttered my father. There was a confused uproar. "Kick them out, boys!" my father shouted. "Ride them out on a rail."

I allowed myself to hope a little. But then a third voice we knew joined in: "George, maybe these men don't mean us any good; I've had my doubts about them for the past two weeks. But you got meat in there and I've only had four pounds this week, for me and my wife and my two kids. Is that Christian? Is that neighborly?"

"I've had less than one pound in two weeks," replied my father. "And my wife has had none, and my boys have had less than I've had. And we have two children at home, too. Listen, boys, listen carefully: though some of you are town-born you know the farmer's lingo, you know his life. And you know you don't eat your seed corn. The farm children are our seed corn, to work on the farm to feed you. If your seed corn dies, you'll die, right here on your streets. You have a chance to live, when the drought and the weeds go, and we get back to working for you."

"You want to live at the expense of the lives of the exploited people," shouted another strange voice.

My father's pale face turned crimson. "You go, dog, with your lies and your plots of disruption. Go home and leave us alone. But be sure we won't forget you."

There came a furious pounding on the door, and my father smiled grimly. He went to the gun rack on the wall, selected a good rifle and examined it. In spite of our desperate situation I could not help smiling at this man of peace who despised violence as the mark of a barbarian.

"We're armed!" cried the leader of the strange voices. "Let us in, or we'll shoot off the locks!"

"No, you won't!" said Joe Schultz, and a wavering chorus of our friends echoed him.

"Are you sheep?" asked the stranger with contempt. "Aren't you entitled to the fruits of the earth, in return for your labor?"

"How many of the swine are they, Joe?" my father called. There was a muttering again, and Joe answered unwillingly: "Three of them, George. And they got pistols. We don't. We don't go around shooting anybody."

"You might try shooting them," said my father, and I smiled again. He said over his shoulder at me, "Call Sheriff Black; tell him professional troublemakers are trying to incite a riot."

I went to the telephone but it was dead. The line must have been cut outside. I told my father. He examined his gun again, and said: "Open the door, Pete. We're going to have a showdown."

But first he tried one last appeal to the people at the doors. "Go home, boys. Go back to your beds. You don't know what you're doing, letting these murderers lie to you and get you out on the streets like hoodlums and gangsters. They just want us all to die, you and me, or to follow them to destruction. Go home."

There was a short, deep silence outside. Then a bullet ripped through our strong door and my father screamed an oath and caught at his left shoulder. I almost dropped my gun in my dread, but he pushed me aside, and with his right hand, he took the heavy iron bolt and pulled it fiercely back. He tore open the door and stood in the doorway, gasping a little, his gun grasped strongly.

The street outside was spectral in the street lights; the yellow moon glimmered in the sky. The townsmen we knew, aghast at the voice of the gun, had drawn back in a knot near the curb. But the three strangers confronted my father with set faces and the leader raised his gun again.

But my father swung his own rifle and knocked the gun out of the other's hand, and then, moving so fast that I could hardly follow him, he grasped the man and pulled him into the warm room, and I slammed the door and shot the bolt. My father flung the stranger onto the floor and set his big foot on his lean belly. "Kill him George," said Sam, in a casual tone. "Shoot his head off."

I put my gun on the table and examined my father's arm. His shoulder was bleeding badly but again he pushed me aside. He pointed the rifle down at the stranger, who was lying still and rigid, staring up into the bole with black, frightened eyes. He was tall and lanky, not more than thirty, with a thin shine of dark hair on his round head. His hands, as they clenched on the floor, were as white as flour.

"Afraid, eh?" asked my father softly. "You'd rather be on my end of the gun wouldn't you? How does it look, son, to stare into the face of death?"

"If you kill me, a defenseless, unarmed man, you'll hang for it," said the stranger harshly.

"Oh, you speak of the law now, do you? And what law permitted you to get those decent men out of bed and lead them to violence? What law told you you could create a riot?"

"I still say, kill him," said Sam, kicking the stranger in the thigh. "Self-defense, George; upholding the law against inciters. The sheriff wouldn't hold you an hour."

"What can you do with such monsters, except kill them?" asked my father. "But when you kill one, a hundred rise up in his place. Don't move, son. What's your name, and where do you come from?"

The man had taken a little courage from what my father had said. He replied in a clear, hard voice: "My name is Will Dowson, an American name, and I come from St. Louis. I'm no farmer, or foreigner, if that's what you want to know." He stared up at my father defiantly.

My father asked in a mild tone: "What made you think I thought you must be a foreigner, son? Don't you think I know that tens of thousands of good Americans are traitors? I see you have a scar on your cheek? Europe? Korea?"

"I was an officer in the American Army, in Korea,"

the stranger answered. His smile was ugly. "I'm not armed, and you three are. Do you mind if I get up? Unless, of course, you intend to kill me after all, in your brutal, savage way."

My father stepped back and said: "Get up. I don't like to see any man on his back—even a man like you." He put his gun on the table and sat down heavily in his chair. I did not like his color, and this time I insisted on examining his shoulder. It was a flesh wound, but it was bleeding freely. I did what I could with it, pressing my handkerchief, rolled into a ball, against the wound. My father hardly noticed me. He was studying our guest, who had seated himself insolently in the one other chair. Watching my father intently, he lit a cigarette.

"I spared your life, boy," my father said. "That won't make you grateful. You think I'm a weakling. In my place, you being so superior and so disciplined and so dedicated, you'd have killed me as you would have killed a dog. Did it ever occur to you that a man might refrain from killing from a moral principle, from a respect of life, even a life like yours?"

Will Dowson sneered. "The future is not for the weak," he said, "nor for superstitious fools who talk about moral law, or principle. Such luxuries have no place in the new order."

"The new order of Russia." My father nodded. I inspected the wound again; it was beginning to clot. I pressed the handkerchief down, hard. "You see, we farmers aren't ignorant peasants, though you people like to think so. You despise us, just as you despise what you call 'the proletariat.' You want to rule us or destroy us, make slaves of us, don't you? You won't; we aren't warbroken Poles or frightened Chinese. We have a tradition of freedom, no matter what we are, or how we work. We might fight among ourselves, but when it comes right down to it, we close ranks as Americans. You can plot and infiltrate, and conspire secretly, and try to undermine our Constitution but you won't get anywhere. We won't let you, no matter what happens."

Again Dowson sneered. His assurance was returning. I took the handkerchief from my father's shoulder and tied the bloody cloth about it carefully. My father was looking steadily at Dowson. "I can't argue with you, I can't convince you. I can't even reach you. And that's a terrible thing, for there are millions like you, everywhere in the world—shut out from reason or mercy or justice."

My father sighed: "The worst part of it is that you believe in your insane religion. And that's where our own guilt comes in. We older people were indifferent about teaching you religion, when you were young. We left a spiritual vacuum, and some kind of perverted religion had to take its place to command your devotion. A man has to have some kind of devotion in his life, some frame of reference, some surety outside himself. That instinct is born in us. Pervert that instinct, deny it, and hell will step in to fill the emptiness that should have been filled with God."

"You gave us a heritage of capitalistic exploitation of the defenseless," said Dowson. He was no longer sneering; a kind of exalted light shone in his black eyes. "You gave us a heritage of superstition and pious lies; you gave us the crisis of all history; you gave us war."

"Yes," said my father, his face devastated. "We gave you war."

"I still say, in spite of this fine talk, that we should kill him," said Sam grimly. "He'll be out of wherever we take him today, doing the same thing in a few hours. Can't you see he hates you, George?"

"Yes," said my father. "And that's why I ask him to forgive me. He has no reason for his hate." He added gravely: "The earth is cursed in him, and in us."

CHAPTER TEN

SHERIFF BLACK booked Dowson on a charge of assault
with intent to kill. Joe Schultz and his town friends,
shocked almost into illness, cooperated with the sheriff,
and the two other strangers were quickly arrested on the
same charge, including a charge of incitement to riot.
Then the sheriff issued an order—which under other cir-
cumstances and in another day would have been immediately upset by the lawyers—that all strangers who had
been in Arbourville for less than three months should
leave within twenty-four hours. "We want no outsiders
here to stir up trouble," said the sheriff. "We have enough
of it ourselves."

My father pleaded for Dowson. He said: "Shelton,
it's all of one piece—these Communist fellows, wars,
drought, the weeds, famine, the 'scorpions,' this damn
queer sun and moon, the earthquakes, the showers of
meteors, the dying children, the sick adults—everything.
They're all a visitation, and every man in the world is
responsible for them."

Shelton Black said he thought this reasoning somewhat

strange. My father explained patiently; the sheriff listened as patiently, and with compassion. He said: "George, I kind of get your idea in a way; after all, I teach a Sunday-school class, don't I? Maybe we all are responsible, as you say, and when I read the Bible to myself at night I get to wondering, too. But I'm a law officer; we've got a man here in jail who tried to kill you and tried to incite a riot. That's the one fact I'm hanging onto; if we start abandoning facts, especially in these days, we're going to have chaos."

My father pointed out that we already had chaos, and that the Government was contributing to it by refusing to admit that the whole nation was in a plight similar to ours here in Arbourville. It, too, was abandoning facts, and so was responsible for the unrest and the terror in the cities, and the belief of the city people that the farmer was hoarding his food for higher prices. The sheriff smiled wryly. "But if we let all the cities know the truth, then we'll see real catastrophe; at least they're being kept in some kind of control now by lies. Perhaps you're right, George, but we still have the fact that a man tried to kill you. I'm sticking to facts. I've got to."

We had no more trouble from the town people after the incident of the Communist-led riot. They were ashamed, and contrite, and Joe Schultz and other grocers and butchers even offered to augment our stock of goods with food from their own shelves. The people approved it with a generosity that was touching. But the farmers refused, saying that in the event their own stocks dwindled to nothing they would call upon the town for help. An air of friendship and kindness developed among all the people, a comradeship in distress.

We noticed that there were no more reports in the press of explosions of atomic or hydrogen bombs any-where in the world. We did hear that Russia had had "an extremely fine harvest" of wheat this year, and that she was shipping her huge surpluses to her satellites. The report had a pathetic sound to it, in spite of the jubilant ring reported in the columns of Pravda. It was curious that Pravda did not mention any "rumors" that the rest of the world was engulfed in a mysterious and deadly vegetation, that famine and plague had broken out everywhere, and that the cities of "the free world" were in a panic. Pravda also ignored the strange sun and moon, the earthquakes and the brilliant cataracts of meteors each night. It was oddly unaware that the desperate Russian farmers, and the farmers in the satellites, were dying by the tens of thousands of starvation and plague and the poisonous creatures in the universal weeds, and that city men and women were being rushed to the land to try to stave off death a little longer.

The great cities of "the free world" celebrated Christmas, of course, though there was a strange absence of metallic toys for the children. Passenger travel between cities for the holiday was extremely light. Even the planes carried very few passengers; it seemed that there were increased movements of the military these days, and the detested word "priority" again crept into the news.

Christmas began dismally enough, under the brazen skies, with the weeds all around and the deadly things they secreted. "Surely, on Christmas, God will have a little mercy on us," said my mother, whose strength was returning very slowly, and whose hair was dead white now. My father shook his head. "Why should He? Have we ever shown any mercy to each other?" But my mother continued to hope.

It was my father's custom to read the account of the Nativity on Christmas Eve. But on this night he opened the Bible to the Book of Job, and we sat about him and listened to the dolorous lamentations of an afflicted man.

"The arrows of the Almighty are within me, the poison whereof drinketh up my spirit; the terrors of God do set themselves in array against me."

I listened, and my old bitterness and rage returned. I could not contain myself and I snatched the book from my father, turned a page or two, and read in a loud and

90

harsh voice: "I will say to God: do not condemn me; tell me why Thou judgest me so. Doth it seem good to Thee that Thou shouldst calumniate me and oppress me, the work of Thy hands, and help the counsel of the wicked? Hast Thou eyes of flesh, or shalt Thou see as man sees? Are Thy days as the days of man, and are Thy years as the times of men: that Thou dost inquire after my iniquity, and search after my sin . . . Thy hands have made me . . . dost Thou thus cast me down? . . ."

I flung the desperately rebuking words of Job to God as Job had flung them. My mother and the girls looked at me with tears in their eyes, and Edward bent his head. But my father, with a sad smile, took the book out of my hands and read:

"Are you then alone, and shall wisdom die with you?"

He regarded me gravely, over his glasses, and I was hot with mortification. Then my father continued: "With the hearing of the ear I have heard of Thee, but now my eye seeth Thee. Therefore I despise myself, and do penance in dust and ashes."

I was suddenly very still. Again, something stirred in my mind, elusive but portentous. I lost myself in urgent search of it, and I started when my father said, leaning towards me: "Yes, Pete?"

"Nothing!" I shouted at him.

I went outside in a turmoil of emotion. Was I losing my mind? I looked up at the sinister stars; I heard the crackling of the weeds, and the foul scuttle among them. My vision blurred with hopelessness. And then it happened.

I was staring at the Milky Way, and suddenly the constellation was no longer a long white scarf in the sky, sprinkled with the diamond points of the rolling suns. It had taken a new shape; it was brightening rapidly, flowing together, distinct and brilliant. A thrill ran through me, and I broke into a cold sweat. I clutched a post of the porch.

A vast cross was forming in the constellation, its outlines clear and sharp and dazzling. It might have taken moments, it might have taken a quarter of an hour. But there it was at last, pure and shining, its topmost part lifted against the farthest reach of the black universe, its arms extended into infinite space. I could not move or stir or cry out. I wanted to kneel; I wanted to weep. But I could only stand there looking incredulously at this mysterious sign, this mysterious message of love and benediction, this mysterious promise.

Then, all at once, it was gone, and the Milky Way was there again, diaphanous and remote.

I shook my head, dazed. Then I ran back into the house. Whom did one call to ask about odd manifestations? The police, the weather bureau, the radio stations? I ran past my family into the sitting room and caught up the telephone, dimly aware that my father and the others were crowding in after me, with alarmed questions. I turned my back to them and called the radio station. The line was busy. I called the police, and the weather bureau. Those lines were busy too. I called our local operator; her line, too, buzzed with frenzy.

My father said sharply: "Pete, what is it? Whom are you calling?"

But I pushed him aside, and turned on our radio. A voice, excited, almost joyous, rushed out to us: "Everyone in the community is calling the police, the radio stations, the weather bureau! Seems some folks around here are positive they saw something in the sky a few minutes ago. Some say it was a cross, some just a blaze, some an extraordinarily large, flaming meteor. The crosses, and not to be irreverent, seem to be the most popular." There was a pause, then the voice said: "I've got a report from the weather bureau, folks. 'Some magnetic disturbance,' it says here. Complicated by distortion. Well, now you know as much as we all do, and why not let up on our telephone?"

I looked at my father, and my trembling must have been visible, for he took my arm strongly: "It was a cross," I said. "A cross, a cross."

My mother burst into tears; Lucy gazed at me, round-

92

eyed; Jean was very pale. Edward, who was usually so silent, said: "I wish I could have seen it." He put his hand up to his clouded glasses.

"Surely," said my father, his blue eyes gentle, "it was a cross."

The house was filled, now, with a sense of peace, of hope. We were weak from our inadequate meals, and our bodies were thin to gauntness. Death waited for us outside, but still peace flowed like cool water over us. We sat down and smiled at each other. "So," said my father, softly, "He hasn't forgotten us."

Our Christmas dinner, consisting of an old rooster and potatoes and apple sauce, was almost hectic with excitement. Many of our neighbors called us to wish us well on the holiday, and a few spoke hesitantly of the rumor of the cross. None of them admitted having seen it himself; he did not wish to seem a fool. But I told what I had seen; my account was received eagerly but also with embarrassment. I had to recount it over and over.

In the evening I climbed into our tractor and went to see our patch of grass. I had not visited it for many weeks, though my father and our tenants cut it regularly. It showed no signs of diminishing; it was as thick and flourishing as ever, free of the poisonous things. It was a pool of sweet light green surrounded by noxious vegetation which dared not intrude upon it. Then I saw something else in its depths. Tiny blue flowers were growing in it, the color and shape of violets. I hurried back to the house and called my father and Edward, and they got into the tractor with me and we went to the patch of grass again. My father got down and picked a few of the flowers; they had a sweet fragrance, penetrating and tender. He put them into Edward's hands.

There was no account at all in any newspaper of the cross in the heavens, but we heard, much later, that it had been seen round the world.

CHAPTER ELEVEN

IN EARLY JANUARY my father received his price-support check and also a check for "drought relief." He looked at the bluish cardboards from Washington, then dropped them into an envelope and sat down and wrote a letter to the Department of Agriculture.

"I am returning to you," he wrote, "your completely worthless checks. I suggest you transform them into one of your wonderful chemicals for raising synthetic vegetables, a project which seems to be occupying all your attention these days.

"The checks are useless, for they will not buy life. You know this, of course. But you send them to persuade each farmer all over the country that his calamity is only a local disturbance confined to his particular area. The farmer is not a fool. He knows that his plight is universal, that there is not a single acre which is cultivable in this country. He knows we are faced with death, and he is beginning to wonder why. He is wondering if he has finally been rejected by the land, and all the cities with him, because of our threatened wars and our bombs and our weapons of destruction.

"He is asking himself why our Government's efforts have not been directed to establishing peace in the world. He is slowly realizing that the business of war is the business of an artificial prosperity, and that so far we have not found a way to full production without the bloody impetus of war."

A week later the telephone rang. Our Senator was calling from Washington. "For God's sake, George," he protested, "what have you been writing to the Department of Agriculture? Never mind how I got the information; you've created a furore—"

"Why?" asked my father, calmly. "I'm just a stock farmer in our state, just one of thousands. How does it happen that I've suddenly become so important?"

The Senator fumed. "George, this is terrible." He paused. "Do the other farmers think the way you do, out there?"

"Well, perhaps not all. But I'm doing my best to convert them to my point of view."

"And what the hell's that?"

"That we've got this death around us because of our everlasting damnable wars, and that we're all guilty of the wars and the political chaos, and that we'll die under the hand of God unless the whole world decides to live in peace."

I was listening in on our upstairs extension, and I heard the Senator make a noise like a strangling man. "Listen to me, George, you're talking in a very dangerous fashion; worse, you're writing in a very dangerous fashion. Now wait a minute. There's someone from Washington going to Arbourville next week to speak to you. George, you'll behave yourself, won't you? I'm your Senator, and your friend—"

"Someone from Washington, eh?" asked my father, with interest. "What does he want? My income tax not made out right?"

He hung up. Edward and I were concerned, but my father laughed at us.

When the agent did arrive in Arbourville and requested an interview, my father suggested he come to our home. But for some reason the man refused. "Afraid of the weeds and the creatures in them?" my father said. "Don't blame you, son. All right, I'll get out the tractor and be in town in a couple of hours."

I went with him, and I urged him to use some restraint. "Hell, this is a free country, isn't it? If it isn't, it's about time we did something about it," my father said.

The man from Washington was owlish and brown and little. He scrutinized my father closely, in the rooms above our post office. "FBI?" asked my father, genially. "Meet my son, Pete. I left my other son at home. You see, he's blind; he gets one hundred and fifty dollars a month, pension. Pretty cheap for a pair of eyes, isn't it?"

Mr. Forbes did not like my father. That was evident immediately. He sat down and looked at his neat stack of papers. "I want to ask you just a few questions, sir," he said. "Father? How many acres? What crops this year? No crops? Well, you've been having a little— difficulty—out here, haven't you? Better next year. Food on hand? Almost nothing? Why did you send the checks back, then?"

"Because I'm a man with a family, and I need bread, not cardboard," said my father. "That's the trouble with all governments these days. Pieces of paper for the price of man's honor and a man's life. Well, time has run out. We're not for sale any more." He was very impatient with the man from Washington. "Come to the point," he said brusquely. "What do you want? I haven't got the time to waste with you."

Mr. Forbes was considerably taken aback by this. He cleared his throat. "Now, sir, just a moment more. You are a farmer, the owner of a medium-sized farm in this state. We respect the farmers—"

"Nice of you," said my father.

96

Mr. Forbes closed his eyes patiently. He repeated: "We respect the farmers. We never have had any quarrel with them. I am only trying to find out why you are discontented, and why you sent back the checks to which you were entitled." He lifted a thin hand. "I am not a member of the Federal Bureau of Investigation. I am only an investigator, one of thousands, sent here to ask you a few questions."

"Well, ask them," my father said.

Mr. Forbes opened his eyes. "If you'll let me, sir," he said sharply. "Were you ever a member of the Communist Party? Are you a member now?"

My father leaned back in his chair. "No, son, I'm a Republican," he replied. "Of course, once in a while I vote for a Democrat I like personally. Is there a new law forbidding you to split your ticket?"

Mr. Forbes sighed. He wrote something on a sheet of paper.

"I was never a Socialist, either," said my father, "and I'm not a temperance man, nor did I ever vote for the Vegetarian Party, or the Free Homes for Everybody Party. That answer your question?"

Mr. Forbes again closed his eyes briefly. I think my father was beginning to enjoy himself. Mr. Forbes said: "You wrote a letter to the Department of Agriculture. In it you expressed a somewhat violent objection to war—"

Suddenly my father leaned forward, his face grim, his eyes bleak. "You're damned right I object to war, and object to war violently. I'm a farmer, and I know what I know. I know we are condemned to death by the earth itself if we don't stop murdering each other. I suppose you've never seen those weeds outside before? I suppose the sun shines bright on Washington, and the parks are green, and the rain is accommodating? I suppose Virginia and Maryland are teeming with good crops, and the winter wheat is coming up, and the warehouses down there are full? I suppose you don't know of a child who died of the plague? And the men and women who are dying of dysentery, you never hear of them either?

97

What about the earthquakes? What earthquakes? You never heard of anything like that, did you?"

He thrust a finger at Mr. Forbes' face. "What's the Government afraid of? Afraid that the people will get the idea they're being punished?"

He stood up. He buttoned his coat, and said to me abruptly: "Let's go, Pete. Mr. Forbes has to fill out his forms, and that'll take him the rest of the day."

I had not had the opportunity to say a single word, nor had I wanted to. I followed my father as he strode ahead of me, big, dauntless, and unafraid.

Edward and Lucy smiled so seldom these days that I could hardly wait to get home and tell them the story of my father and the man from Washington. He, himself, had already forgotten. He struggled mightily with the heaving tractor on the way home. He might be emaciated, but he was a man of the earth and still full of strength.

I never did get around to telling my brother and his wife the story. We arrived home to find the household in disorder. My little boy had been stung by a "scorpion," and he was dying.

He had been an amiable little fellow almost from the hour of his birth. Even now, at the age of eighteen months, he did not cry too often with hunger. He had the bright, blue, piercing eyes of my father, the sweet disposition of my mother, and her round face and curling chestnut hair. He would play alone in his crib for hours, chuckling and gurgling in the unknown tongue of babies. He was intelligent and gay and content, and the joy of the family, and Lucy and Edward loved him as well as they loved their remaining child. He had been named after my father, who adored him. He found everything interesting and exciting, from a streak of sunshine to Jean's eyelashes. We called him Porgie.

Distraught, my mother told us what had happened. The house, guarded as it was, constantly searched as it was, had been invaded by one of the monstrous things.

How it had got upstairs we never knew. But it had found Porgie and it had stung him, while Jean had been out of the room for just a moment. My mother, usually timid and fearful, had looked for it and had discovered it under the crib. In spite of her loathing and her horror, she had managed to kill it. It lay crushed on the floor.

It had happened less than five minutes before we got home. I found Jean, white-lipped and blank-eyed, frantically applying hot compresses to the child's heel. I got to work with the swiftness of desperation. There were ways of dealing with snakes; I ran for my razor, and, holding the child as he sobbed in agony, I made a gash in the wound and I put my mouth to it and sucked. I put a tourniquet about his soft little leg and tightened it. Then I loosened the knot and tightened it again, forcing the wound to bleed. The baby, after a struggle or two, and several screams, became ominously quiet, breathing convulsively in my arms. A purplish shadow crept over his face; he began to gasp for breath. It had been too late from the beginning.

Slowly Porgie's eyes became glazed. His breath was shallow now. He fixed his eyes on me, unseeing, and I held him to me tightly. Then I knew I was holding a dead child. But still I held him, murmuring to him. Jean uttered a single, sharp cry, and collapsed.

It was my father who took the baby from me, and laid him gently in his crib. I watched, in dull and unbelieving anguish. My father covered him with a blanket and shut his eyes. "Porgie, Porgie," he said, and his voice broke and his eyes ran with tears.

Then he turned to me and said: "Pete, take care of Jean. Comfort her. And try not to forget that you'll have another child in five months. Jean needs you now."

She was sitting in a chair, her head hanging over the side, and the soft dark hair I loved covered her face and dangled down her arm. I tried to get up to go to her, but I fell back, and it seemed to me that my life was running out through my hands and fingers. Then my father was pressing a glass of whisky against my mouth and

99

forcing me to drink it. "The poison may kill you, too," he said, sternly. "Drink this down, at once."

I drank, mechanically. I heard a rough, gasping sound in the room, and it was some time before I recognized it as my own breathing. I went to Jean, now, and I fell on my knees beside her and put my head on her shoulder, weeping aloud. She did not move. My mother smoothed her hair, but it was as if she herself had died.

Then I felt Edward's hand on me, and he was saying in a kind, slow voice: "Pete, we lost our boy, too. It was almost impossible to stand, but we stood it. There'll be two more babies in the house, soon. It's poor comfort, I know, but it's all we have."

I could not reconcile myself to Porgie's death. It was a barbarous and evil thing, and God had inflicted it upon us. For a time I became a complete atheist. Life was intolerable; life had been made intolerable by God. He had had no mercy upon this little boy who had done no harm. It was not until our new doctor told me that Jean was in danger of losing the baby she carried that I rallied a little for her sake.

She was ill until the end of January, lying in bed with a closed and apathetic face. My mother boiled some of our last chickens for her and fed her as if she were a child. When I sat beside her I would take her hand; it was cold and lifeless and she would turn her head away from me. Once she said: "If you had been at home—if you had been at home, it would never have happened. I had to leave him alone for just a minute and you know I never left him unless you could take my place."

My father, who was there then, said: "Jean, it happened all at once. Even if you had been sitting there you couldn't have saved him. Look at poor Pete." I began to curse the man from Washington who had called us away. I cursed the weeds and the "scorpions" and I cursed God. Never had I been so engulfed in hatred and pain.

I did not notice that no snow came, that the heat did not slacken, and that death marched unrelentingly over

100

the countryside. I did what work there was to do, and I became as quiet as Edward. The foul creatures in the weeds did not disappear. My only pleasure—vindictive, almost rapturous—was in killing them, in hunting them out for hours at a time.

It was February now, and the weeds were as high as our hips, and there was no rain, no sign of spring, no sweetness in the air. One night I said to my father: "We might as well give up. We are going to die sooner or later, and it might as well be sooner."

For the first time we had to go to the Grange in Arbourville and get our rations. Most of our fowl and our cows, and all but three of our pigs, had died.

Then the cities, in their witless terror, erupted into murderous panic.

CHAPTER TWELVE

As WE LIVED in an inland community we had no access to any body of water larger than our little Lake Wilde, which had never been abundantly stocked with fish. Our other sources of water were the brooks and narrow streams, now almost dry, and few fish ever had traversed them except during the spring floods. When the fish had disappeared last summer it had not caused much comment except among those who had time for fishing, and our family was not among them.

Of course, the newspapers and other sources of public information did not let us know that in communities blessed with huge bodies of water the fish had gone entirely. Worst of all, we found out later that the sea had refused to give up her creatures to the nets and the trawlers. The oysters vanished, and the shrimp and the clams and the lobsters, and though fishing boats went dangerously far out into the oceans to cast their nets they pulled in few if any edible fish.

We know now that the countries who subsist largely on fish were the most desperately stricken of all of us.

Millions died of starvation in Scandinavia alone, and millions died in Britain too, long before the rest of the world was seriously afflicted. The inland countries were still eating meat then. It is to the credit of Scandinavia and Britain that their people did not riot first. But American people rioted in full mass while there were still some canned vegetables and meat in the markets, and some flour and corn and potatoes. And it is to our shame that the news of our rioting spread to other afflicted countries and set them off.

To people accustomed to unlimited meat and milk and fruits and butter, to exotic canned goods, to green vegetables and orange juice and "balanced diets," the situation had become outrageous and maddening. "Mothers' movements" sprang up overnight, led by fierce-eyed strangers, little women who were not mothers at all, and had no prospects of becoming mothers. Banners, lettered in red, appeared suddenly and copiously from nowhere, screaming: "Our children want milk! Our children demand fresh fruits and vegetables! Our children must have meat! We demand action! The Government must act!"

"Workers' Movements" roared into being, led by the male counterparts of the hectic little women. The appeared, as if at a signal, haranguing the men as they came out of the factories or the mills or the shops. The Government warehouses were "bulging," they shouted. They were cracking at the seams with hoarded butter and meat and wheat and corn, bought from "selfish, greedy, special interests," and kept from "the people" for higher prices. Capitalism was the culprit. Under a fair system of government food would be plentiful for "the masses, the exploited worker." A planned economy must be put into operation at once.

We heard later that mobs composed of tens of thousands of men and women, led by the strangers, stormed the city warehouses, killed or trampled the guards, and poured in demented hordes through the empty buildings. The emptiness brought them momentarily to a standstill. They stared about them in the hollow silence of the

103

warehouses. But the leaders had a quick explanation. The Government had secretly restored the goods to the "fat farmers" in order to keep them from the cities until higher prices were permitted. The land, cried the strangers, was not producing for use. It was producing for profits.

The governors of the states called out the National Guard, and then appealed desperately to the President for the Army. For two weeks the soldiers were able to prevent the populace of the cities from flowing out into the countryside like a devouring forest fire. They set up huge guns on the outskirts and made it clear that the guns would be used if necessary.

In the meantime, news of our rioting cities reached Europe. London went mad; Paris mobs streamed through the streets by day and by night, looting, burning, destroying. There was not a city which did not lose its mind, anywhere in the world, including Russia.

Congress was called into emergency session. The President addressed it. He pleaded with all members to go back to their constituents and reason with them. But the members of Congress looked back at the President with haunted eyes, and did not obey. They were afraid, now, of their own people, and of questions they could not answer.

The cities, taking breath for the last fatal onslaught, panted behind their barriers of steel. Soldiers did not dare to appear alone on the streets, or even in couples. The police had disappeared. Martial law was declared. Curfews were announced. But it was impossible, and it would have been unpardonable, to shoot down the thousands of paraders who defied the military, even led as they were by the strangers. The Army tried shutting off electricity at night, and so keeping the streets black. The people were amazingly, and promptly, armed with torches. They eddied and flowed and streamed through the streets, the torchlight reflecting redly from the sides of buildings. Millions paraded and screamed and threatened with raised, clenched fists.

The small towns and the villages did not riot, for they

were too close to the country, and there the people knew the truth.

Frustrated in their urge to inundate the countryside, the mobs turned their rage on their own means of existence, the factories and the mills. Countless millions of dollars' worth of property was destroyed in twenty-four hours, before the Army could intervene.

The clergy attempted pacification, but as they had been warned not to tell the real truth, their attempts failed. They talked sternly or soothingly of the "need to maintain order." They talked of God, not as an affronted and angry God, but as a source of infinite mercy in whom the people could put their hope. They left their churches and talked on the streets, in the scarlet shadow of torchlight or under the day's yellow skies. The people did not listen. They howled their derision at priest and minister and rabbi, and drowned out their voices. In many instances these innocent and pleading men were trampled by the mobs or were beaten to death.

All the mills and the factories were closed. The banks closed, one by one. And then the churches closed. There were no people who wished to go to church, anyway. It happened all over the civilized world.

The markets were empty, everywhere. What little had remained in them had been seized by the insane mobs. There was, now, nothing for the people to eat, except the small stores they had on their own shelves, and these were dwindling fast.

It is to the credit of humanity, everywhere, that the men who maintained the utilities remained on their jobs, though they were starving. Otherwise millions would have died of thirst.

The United Nations met in extraordinary session during the last days of February. By this time the cities had found arms.

CHAPTER THIRTEEN

LESTER HARTWICK, our Grange president, called my
father. He was asking all local farmers to come to the
Grange hall for consultation and information that night.
We went there, greeted our gaunt friends, and waited.
An air of doom and despondency hovered in the hall.

Lester said: "We've had some confidential news about
the cities. They're rioting. Martial law's been declared;
the Army is out." He was so weak that he paused between sentences, and kept running his hand dazedly over
his face. "Now, Grovetown is only one hundred miles
from here—eight hundred thousand people. They can
get around to this community in less than three hours,
for the highways are still open. They're already talking
about it; we're the richest farming community in this part
of the state. The city people know all about the Grange
stocks of food for the farmers."

He stopped again, and looked at us with haggard eyes.
"Boys, we've got our seed corn and wheat piled up here,
waiting for when we can plant it again. I want you all
to take it away; it's the only chance for food for the

future for all of us. Turn the weeds over with your tractors, far from your houses; bury the seed deep, mark the place. The weeds will grow over it in a few hours. Make sure you line the hole with wood or concrete; I don't know how much time we have now.

"And then, divide what we have here on hand among yourselves, all the food and meat. Take it home; hide it away. I don't think you'll have to worry much; they'll attack the Granges first. But arm yourselves. Boys, this is war, not to kill people but to save them, the poor damn fools.

"The mayor of Arbourville is here tonight. He wants to offer us the big factory which used to be the silk mills, until the owners moved south. Start bringing your cattle and hogs and other stock here tomorrow, at dawn. Get them here as soon as you can. The factory's at the edge of town, and nobody goes there any more. Here in Arbourville we'll take the hay and the corn to the factory, for the stock.

"Grange presidents all over the country have made these plans. Now, go home, and come back tomorrow with your trucks and tractors. There's no time to be lost."

We spent four hours portioning out the food for ourselves. Those who had children and pregnant wives were given the largest shares. We worked in the steaming heat, with the strength born of fear and dread. We loaded our seed corn and wheat in bags; it was good to look at the seed again, hard and yellow and dry in our hands, the fruit of life, the promise of life. We worked, not only for ourselves, but for all men.

My father and I reached home in the saffron dawn, ate hastily, and then took our tractor out. We tore at the weeds, ripping them up, our tractor grinding and crushing. The murky sun was hot on our backs by the time we had made a large enough hole. We lined it with thick wood and tossed our bags into it, and sealed it. It would keep for several months, we hoped. Within a few hours the weeds had grown back over the place; we set a marker on the spot, unobtrusive to any eyes but our own.

It was not until the next dawn that we could load our remaining two cows, the bull, and the three pigs, into our truck. When we reached the abandoned mills in Arbourville we found them already teeming with bellowing, frightened stock. The citizens of the town had been working without sleep; hay and corn filled improvised bins, and barrels of water were placed at intervals. It was a lonely place; the factory had broken windows, but the doors were strong and several of the townsmen offered to stand guard inside. It would not be safe for them to be seen outdoors.

We hid our food in our empty barns, under hastily ripped-up floors, under eaves, under beds, in blind attics reached by ladders. We had to live, if any other men were to live.

My father was contained and steadfast during all this, but my disgust and hatred for mankind was growing. In my exhausted and grief-stricken mind the men of the cities, men everywhere, were responsible for my child's death. I made a solemn vow that if my family were spared I would never again lift a hand to help others, no matter how needy or hopeless. In that way, I told myself, I would escape future agony.

After we had completed our almost superhuman work we sat down to wait. My father was full of assurance, as always. We had not been talking to each other much these days, and when I sat down in the sitting room I picked up a book. I knew he was watching me, as he smoked. Then he said: "Pete, I have an idea what's bothering you, and giving you that bitter expression. It's Porgie. You've worked with all of us, and buried the seed corn and wheat, and taken only your just share of the food. But you always looked as if you were doing it unwillingly. I think you've been cursing your fellowmen, deep inside you."

I did not answer him. I heard him sigh. "Pete, I hate to say this, but you aren't any better than your neighbor. You're no worse, perhaps, but you're no better. A man doesn't stand alone, even when he is the most lonely and keeps his doors shut tight. He is only a part of mankind; he couldn't live without it."

"I'm not interested any longer in my neighbor," I said, curtly. "I feel he is guilty of Porgie's death." I dropped the book and stared at my father, and my heart began to beat with sudden violence. Then I stood up.

"You've remembered something," said my father.

I was unbearably excited. "I have!" Then I stopped. What idiocy! "Lord, have mercy upon me, a sinner." Those were the words of the prayer I had forgotten. I remembered them now, but the passion I had felt when uttering them so long ago was gone. The sick weight of resentment and hate was too strong in me. The patch of grass had been a strange accident.

My father was standing up; he was approaching me almost on tiptoe, for fear that I would forget again. He whispered: "Pete, Pete. The prayer!"

I told him, and I blushed self-disgust at my sentimentality. "It couldn't have been that," I said.

But my father was already running to the telephone, and he was calling young Mr. Herricks. I began to swear, more and more embarrassed. I went upstairs to see Jean. She seemed better, and smiled wanly at me, and kissed me. She was sitting in a chair, and as I stood beside her she held my hand, tightly. She was so pale and thin, so listless.

"Darling, you look so grim these days that you frighten me," she said. Her voice broke. "I know you think about Porgie. But we're going to have another baby—"

I had forgotten the sudden hideous danger which threatened my wife, and Lucy, who were carrying whatever future there would be within their bodies. Now I thought of the insane city mobs pouring out into the country. They would have no mercy on these girls; the least they would do would be to deprive them of our last store of food. I went to my chest of drawers and took out my gun. I went into the clothes closet and got my rifle. I gathered all my ammunition together. If we were injured, if our food was menaced, then I would

109

shoot to kill. I fingered the triggers of the weapons and I almost hoped I would have an opportunity to use them.

"Peter," said Jean, faintly, raising herself a little in her chair. "What is it? Pete, you look so—awful. As if you want to kill."

"I do," I said, before I could stop myself.

She sank back into her chair and looked at me with eyes that were prominent in her thin white face. She began to speak softly, watching me every moment: "I think I have some idea, Pete. But haven't you forgotten something? The cross on Christmas Eve."

"The cross!" I laughed shortly. "I imagined it. Just a magnetic disturbance—that's what they said, wasn't it?"

"But you saw it, Pete!"

I was silent. I could see, again, the infinite and brilliant cross against the black night. I had seen it, myself. I put away the gun and the rifle, and suddenly I was overcome with weakness. I knelt down beside Jean and put my head into her lap. She touched me with tender hands. "Poor Pete, poor darling," she murmured.

Much of my grief and all of my hatred and contempt left me.

"Surely goodness and mercy shall follow me all the days of my life," whispered Jean, and she held my head against her breast.

The yellow light at the windows began to fade as the evening came. I remained with Jean, too exhausted to speak or move. She slept in her chair and I thought that some color was returning to her face. I still could not look without anguish at the empty crib between the ruffled curtains at the windows. What was to become of all of us? How much longer had we to live? Two children would be born again in this house; how were they to survive? But still, a dull peace had come to me.

Mr. Herricks came that night, brought to us by a neighbor's belching tractor. We had not seen him for some time, and I was aghast at the change in him. He seemed weary and broken and very sad. Yet, as he shook

110

my hand he smiled at me, and his youthful eyes became radiant. He had brought his own food with him, and my mother and Lucy prepared it and we all sat down together for our sparse meal. He told us that very few people, if any, came to church now. Either they were dead or dying, sick or desolate, unable to travel even a little distance, or nursing their children or their parents. He visited them in their homes, giving them what comfort he could. He looked at me directly, now. "The gospel of repentance," he said. "How can I say to them: 'Pray for forgiveness'? Wouldn't it be cruel? But that is the only prayer which will save the world now. True repentance, true penance. It has seemed strange to many people that when Christ cured the blind and the lame He usually told them that their sins had been forgiven them. What had affliction to do with sin? Besides, there was evidence all about us that the wicked appeared to be especially blest; their affairs prospered, their children were happy, they were honored among men, they died with at least as much serenity as good men. The charitable and the just, on the other hand, seemed to be the most unlucky of people."

He still gazed at me, but I was confused. "It is not new that men confuse material prosperity with blessedness, and fail to value spiritual prosperity."

These were strange and humble words from our "educated parson," who had once given us fine and scholarly lectures on ethics and psychiatry and world politics and the origins of various philosophies.

There seemed to be some sort of conspiracy between him and my father. When it was dark they both invited me to come out with them in the tractor. We lumbered through the crawling and writhing weeds, which tried to grasp our vehicle in their thorned branches. Above us, the terrible orange moon stared at the earth in unrelenting malignance; from its face there seemed to be flowing the breath of death, foul with corruption. But Mr. Herricks looked up at it with serene calm, and his lips moved without sound.

111

We reached the patch of grass. I had never been here at night, and I was astonished to see that here the yellow moonlight, which lay in ochre reflections on the broad leaves of the weeds surrounding the patch, was a gentle, cool silver. The tall grass was the most beautiful and comforting sight in the world, softly stirring in the night wind, touched with an illumination I had never thought to see again. Mr. Herricks and my father stepped down into its fragrant depths, and when their heels crushed some of the blades a sweet perfume rose from them, a perfume I remembered with sharp and nostalgic sorrow. Then I saw that the two men were looking at me expectantly, and I climbed down and stood beside them. Mr. Herricks was very pale in the moonlight. He held out his hands, and we took them, and then we knelt with him in the grass.

He lifted his face without fear to the moon, and said aloud, in a clear strong voice, "Oh, Lord our God, we stand indicted before Thee as evil men, as guilty men, men without charity or mercy, men without wisdom or kindness. We have disdained Thy word, or mocked it; we are a generation without faith—savage, cruel, bloodthirsty. Though many generations have passed since the day when Thou didst climb the Mount of Calvary, never has there been a race like unto us. We have spread desolation on Thy gentle earth; we have devastated the life-giving fields, and crushed the homes of the helpless. We have taught our children hatred and lust, wars and wicked philosophies. We have never sought peace or conciliation, for these did not bring us profit. The world has not known our like before."

He raised his hand to the dark sky in which the moon was like a wound.

"There is no man without guilt in this world, not even those dedicated to Thy service. We have been false shepherds. We have no defense. We have abandoned the Way of the Cross, we led our flocks not beside the green pastures and the still waters, but into death. We are the guilty. In our guilt is the guilt of all mankind."

112

He was weeping now without concealment. He stretched out his arms and cried: "God, be merciful to me, a sinner!"

My father, kneeling there beside him, lifted up his own arms and prayed: "God, be merciful to me, a sinner."

I thought of all the wild and blasphemous thoughts I had had since the day my child had died. I thought of the weapons I had held and how I had longed to use them in revenge. I was sick with self-loathing. I cried out: "God, be merciful to me, a sinner!"

For a long time we knelt in the darkness, our heads bent, the sweet grass rustling about us. We thought our own wretched thoughts, and over and over we pleaded that mercy be extended to us, not that we might be permitted to live, but that we might be forgiven. Life was no longer of importance, nor physical suffering, nor the thought of death.

We stood up at last, shaken and silent. But a great peace filled us, a sense of pardon, of consolation. We smiled at each other. There was no more terror in us, or dread. We had prayed, and we had been forgiven.

Then Mr. Herricks uttered a great and ringing cry. He was pointing at the ground. And now we saw that the weeds had gone, utterly, completely, for as far as our eye could see in the moonlight. A field of soft and shallow green extended about us, silvery and living. The stench of death had been sucked away, and the blessed fragrance of life rose in the air.

We began to run, crazily, crying aloud, bending to touch the new grass, the warm and crumbling earth. My father threw himself on his knees and kissed the grass and the ground; he fondled the blades in his big hands. He laughed and shouted and cried incoherently. We could not have enough of it. I rolled in it, without fear, knowing that no stinging death was hiding there. I grasped handfuls of the soil, let it sift slowly through my fingers. It was moist and fresh, eager for seed. Tomorrow I would plough it, tomorrow I would scatter the seed!

Mr. Herricks stood in the midst of the grass and lifted his arms to the heavens. "Thou hast not abandoned Thy children! Blessed be the name of the Lord!" His voice rang over the field like an exultant bell. "Blessed be the name of the Lord!"

CHAPTER FOURTEEN

THE NEXT MORNING we discovered that our entire farm had been cleared of the malignant weeds, up to the very fences of our neighboring farms, to the roads, up to and including our orchards. It was incredible; my father and I walked over our soft and greening acres, dazed. Then the birds came, thousands of them screaming, whistling, singing, chattering excitedly, settling in the grass to hunt for worms. Everywhere endless hordes of them descended upon us, brushing our heads and shoulders, swinging in clouds against the sky, fluttering down in a storm of feathers. The rabbits came, and the foxes, and the squirrels and the woodchucks, running across our feet, staring at us with wild eyes of delight, gamboling in the grass, rolling and jostling each other. A starved buck and two does crept timidly out, glancing about them, then stopped to eat, voraciously. None feared us; they stood with us, and we with them. My father smiled, but tears ran down his face.

We went to the orchard, and we saw the buds on the trees. They had appeared in a single night, thrusting and vigorous. Where the weeds had swarmed, the soil lay crumbling and rich. But when we reached the fences and looked at our neighbors' land we saw again the arching weeds, rapacious and deadly, waving in the murky sunlight.

Within two hours the farmers had gathered on our land. They came from everywhere. They stood and gazed in reverent awe at the greening sod, ran it through their fingers, wept, rubbed blades of grass between their palms, smelled it, holding it close to their noses to inhale the fragrance. They brought a few emaciated cattle to graze, and they laughed shakily to see the poor beasts snorting and chewing and trembling with joy. Then they questioned us. My father said: "Wait. You'll hear about it later." He glanced at me mysteriously.

The newspapers sent out reporters with cameras. They came on tractors, and then walked carefully over the yielding earth. They talked eagerly to my father, and he repeated: "Wait."

My mother and the girls laughed together, and cried. They brought out Edward's little boy, whose short memory did not extend back before the weeds. He toddled over the swift-growing grass, and laughed at the birds and the animals. He picked the first buttercups we saw, and ran to us with them, jabbering with excitement. We could actually see the grass grow, and the flowers between the blades. And then out of nowhere appeared swarms of bees, the lost bees we had forgotten. They hummed over the flowers and the grass, falling and rising in great golden clouds.

All our land was filled with the birds and the beasts and the bees, and with strolling and praying farmers. At ten o'clock young Mr. Herricks arrived, pale and smiling. A few moments later Sheriff Black arrived, with deputies guarding the three strangers who had assaulted the Grange and had attempted to kill my father. The sheriff looked about him dumbly, forgetting his prisoners for a moment. Like the others, he knelt and touched the soil and looked at the bees and laughed shakily in order to

116

keep himself from crying. Then he said to my father: "Well, George, I've brought the rascals, like you asked. What for? Look at them, sneering together, and so damned superior!"

The three young men, scowling and whispering and smirking, stood at a distance with the deputies.

A signal must have been exchanged between my father and Mr. Herricks. The young minister lifted up his hand and called to the farmers. They came, stepping softly over the grass; the sheriff herded his prisoners and deputies together. Mr. Herricks and my father and I stood in the midst of a wide circle, the newspaper men hovering about snapping photographs. And all around us the jubilant song of life rose in a quickening chorus.

Mr. Herricks' voice rang out over the busy acres, the perfumed acres. He said, and his face gleamed with exaltation: "Last night a miracle was performed, before my eyes. Last night our friend and neighbor, George, and his son, Peter, prayed with me. And immediately after we prayed God granted us the miracle we see about us now."

There was a sudden, absolute silence. Each man strained toward us, listening. And then Will Dowson, the man had shot my father, cried out: "Idiotic nonsense! What chemical did you use? Why has it been withheld?"

Mr. Herricks turned slowly and gaped at the prisoners. The farmers murmured in ugly undertones, but the minister lifted his hand and said: "The chemical of prayer, young man."

Dowson pushed closer to him, animated with scorn and anger. "You pious hypocrite. Somehow this farmer either manufactured a chemical himself, or it was secretly given to him for experimentation by an oppressive government—"

"Shut up!" shouted a few farmers, and now the murmur had a murderous sound to it. But neither Mr. Herricks nor Dowson was distracted. They confronted each other steadfastly.

117

"You will never believe anything kind or charitable about your neighbor," said Mr. Herricks, sadly. "You are filled with hatred. It was your hatred for us, and our hatred for you, which evoked the wrath of God against all of us. It was our mutual hatred, our lack of compassion and understanding, which cursed the earth for our sakes. There was no end to our hatred. And there was no end to the death. Until today."

He approached Dowson until they stood face to face. "We are more guilty, even than you," he said. "We, the shepherds, did not go out to find you in the barren desert where you lived. We just waited in our churches for you to come. We acceded to the demand of our enemies that the name of God be forbidden within the walls of your class-rooms. Lost and lonely in your concrete wilderness, where were you to go? The shepherd's voice was absent; his rod and his staff lay hidden and idle in his church. There was no one to comfort you, or lead you to the green valleys of consolation. You were surrounded by ravening beasts, and we closed our eyes and pretended they did not exist.

"For that we were punished, both victims together. For that, we must know and acknowledge our repentance. For that we must pray: God, be merciful to me, a sinner."

He turned from Dowson and looked at all the farmers. "There is not a man here who is not guilty of the crimes of all of us, whether it be the crime of a government against its people, the crime of a pastor who deserted his flock, the crime of hatred against a neighbor. Where is the voice that cried: 'Thou shalt not kill?' Where is the man who had courage to say: 'I shall not take arms against my brother?'

"There was never such a voice, never such a man, in this day. For that we must repent, or we shall die. And after our repentance we must do penance. It is hard for us to love mankind, for mankind has demonstrated that it is unworthy of love. Yet, we must do the penance of loving our neighbors.

"It is too late for lip service, the service of the Pharisee. God is deaf to such prayers. There must be an awakening in the hearts of man, true repentance, true penance. Not prayers that we be saved from the death of the body, but prayers that we be saved from the death of the spirit, which is hatred and lust and cruelty and materialism."

Now from the farmers rose a single deep and resonant voice: "Amen."

Will Dowson was no longer sneering, but his face was like stone. "Give me a demonstration," he said. "Show me that a God exists."

Mr. Herricks turned to my father, who nodded. The pastor said: "Let us go to the next farm. Let us stand near the weeds. But let no man come with us who disbelieves, who is skeptical, except this one stranger among us."

We walked over the shining acres, a stream of pilgrims, in deep silence. We reached the east border of our farm. In spite of all that had happened, I was uneasy. Would God permit another miracle? I glanced back at the men behind me, at the newspaper reporters and photographers, who were almost dancing with excitement.

Mr. Herricks walked fearlessly among the tearing weeds, and my father and I walked with him. We stood knee-deep among them. Mr. Herricks' lips were moving, and he was very pale. He said, and his voice was loud and clear in the silence: "Let us pray together."

He lifted his hands to the sky: "Lord our God, Lord our Father, have mercy upon Your children. Look at our repentance, our tears. If it be Your will, we shall die humbly, in punishment for the sins which we acknowledge. But if it be Your will to grant us life, then we shall rejoice and shall teach our children Your name each day that we live, and we shall drive our hatred for each other out of our hearts, and shall lay down our arms and strive to love and understand each other."

The farmers listened and they cried, and they called again: "Amen!" But Will Dowson stood apart with a closed face, staring at the weeds.

We waited in absolute silence. The loathsome vegetation stood in thick defiance as far as we could see. Endlessly it crackled and snapped. There would be no miracle. I looked at Mr. Herricks, who was gazing at the monstrous growth humbly, and with faith.

Was it the wind that was stirring? We could hear movement, like a gale through dry brush. The heat was intense, the stench overpowering. A vast sulphurous exhalation almost smothered us.

There would be no miracle.

No one moved or spoke.

The crackling grew louder until it sounded like a forest fire, and some of us looked about fearfully for wisps of smoke. Yes, the weeds were smoking; a drift of vapor moved over them, thickened, spread, until they were concealed in a whitish fog, in the folds of which the yellowish sunlight glimmered. Far and wide the vapor drifted under the saffron sky, billowing, swelling, streaming into the distance, hiding the weeds which I now knew were the visible manifestation of our universal hatred. It flowed about trees, climbed distant knolls, sank into small depressions, eddied and swirled. We watched it petrified, almost disbelieving.

And then we shouted out in one single cry. The vapor nearest us was retreating like a silent, misty tide. And where it retreated the warm brown earth steamed, cleansed of its evil. It must have taken a long time, though we were all still and motionless after that one bursting cry. We could do nothing but watch as the nearer ground softened with a misty green and then seemed to run after the retreating fog in its own gentle tide of life.

The farmers, unable to control themselves any longer, broke and ran, laughing and shouting, over the yielding earth, stopping to embrace each other for a quick instant before running again. Their voices echoed round and about. They bellowed for plows, for seed. A hysteria of joy and ecstasy possessed them. And we—Mr. Herricks, Father and myself, and Sheriff Black and Will Dowson—remained behind. The newspaper men pursued

120

the delirious farmers, snapping pictures, questioning each other excitedly, leaping small furrows like children.

Mr. Herricks turned to the prisoner, who stood in complete and disbelieving rigidity. His eyes were blank. When Mr. Herricks spoke he swung his head in his direction, and waited dumbly.

"Here, in the sky, and here, in the earth, is your certitude," said our pastor. "Here is that which you have sought all your life and never found. Your God, your Father." He held out his hand and smiled. "Forgive me, brother."

EPILOGUE

"Why sleep ye? Rise and pray."

THE NEWSPAPERS went mad with joy, amazement and
wonder, as the clergy prayed among the weeds, their
flocks about them, and as the earth miraculously cleared
and the green tide of life flowed over the land and the
trees blossomed and the sweetness of the new resurrection
filled the air with fragrance. Scientists, disbelieving,
toured the country, to return to Washington awed and
humbled. The whole nation prayed with deep repentance and deep rejoicing, and the farmers set their crops
and the wheat and the corn grew so rapidly and with
such abundant power that it was almost possible to see
them grow, shining in the untainted sunlight, glimmering
under the moon. The livestock, too, as if seized by a
mysterious creative power, reproduced in incredible
numbers, and fattened, and reproduced again, even out
of season.

The news had spread rapidly to other nations, whose

governments were at first skeptical and derisive, and whose newspapers spoke darkly of "a secret method invented by scientists in the United States to clear the land," a secret, they declared, that the American "imperialists" would not divulge to other, desperate people. It was a plot, some of them hinted, to starve the rest of the world and leave the United States as the sole living member of the family of nations.

But the people, as usual, were wiser than their governments and their newspapers. In England, France, Germany, Italy, Canada, Scandinavia, South America, Australia, in almost every land of the world, the people, led by their pastors, boldly tramped through the monstrous weeds and lifted their eyes to the sky, and humbly confessed their guilt and prayed for forgiveness. And wherever they confessed and prayed, the land gushed into life and the weeds blew away in vapor and the trees blossomed and flying creatures returned, with all the living things which had hidden themselves from death and the cruelty of man.

"We are Thy fold, and Thou art our shepherd!" men cried to the heavens. "Look, Thou in mercy on our sins and accept our tears and contrition, and wash our hearts clean of our hatred in the river of Thy love, and, if it be Thy will, permit us to live to speak of Thy glory and Thy compassion."

In nearly every land the clergy and the people prayed, and in India the monks in their saffron gowns led fearless multitudes into the very depths of the weeds and prayed for mercy, and confessed, in a great single voice, their sins and their faithlessness. And the weeds fled from mountains and the waters of the rivers ran clean and brilliant under a fresh sun, and the earth lifted her green face to God and man, smiling.

It did not happen in a day, or a month. It happened slowly over nearly a year, except in Russia. The President of the United States declared a day of rejoicing, to be celebrated with humility and love and peace, and one by one the presidents and rulers of other nations followed his example. But Russia was silent, except for her newspapers, who raised the cry of a plot to destroy her. In the United Nations, to rows of sad and averted faces, she accused the delegates of other nations of refusing to give their secret to her in order that she might live.

Then one of the American delegates rose and said quietly, "Disarm, free your people, return to God, confess your sins, as we did, and do penance, as we did. Come with us into the presence of God."

"The doctrines of Marx—" began one of the Russian delegates, looking about him with a starved, gray face, but the American delegate interrupted, "Have those doctrines cleared your land and restored life to your people? Read his doctrines to the weeds, and let them answer you."

"Let our scientists examine your ground for your mysterious, secret chemicals," said the Russian delegates, and smiled knowingly. So the Russian scientists were granted this permission, and returned to their masters in awed silence.

In mercy, the other nations offered to ship huge loads of grain and meat to Russia. They expected refusal and vilification, but, to their surprise and happiness, the delegates accepted the offers. When other nations, shortly afterwards, beamed powerful messages to the people of Russia and the satellite states, the Kremlin said nothing.

The silence behind the Iron Curtain became even more impenetrable, and now no refugees escaped from behind it to tell what was happening in Russia, and what the people were thinking. All at once, however, the Kremlin announced that no further shipments of food would be accepted from the free world. The United Nations was filled with consternation and pity.

The President suggested that representative clergy of all nations appear in the United Nations building to lead the delegates in prayer and thanksgiving. On Christmas Day the clerical delegations arrived, rejoicing. It had been expected that the Russian delegates would absent themselves, but to the amazement of all they were in their seats, smiling faintly. Some thought they smiled in derision.

The services of thanksgiving were about to begin when the Russian delegates and the delegates of their satellite states rose in a body, and silence fell over the assemblage. Were these men, as usual, about to create a disturbance by their protests? Every anxious eye fixed itself upon them, as they stood in a portentous phalanx.

"We wish the services to be delayed for a few moments," said the leader. He lifted his hand in a signal, and remained standing among his fellows. An intense air of suspense settled on the assembly.

Then into the crowd there came the Grand Prelate of Russia, followed by his lesser clergy, and from among the welter of brilliant color and lace and white robes and reverent faces rose a Byzantine crucifix. Delegates of all nations rose with one movement, listening in astonishment to the chant of the Russian priests, a chant of thanksgiving and joy. Disbelieving, the other delegates watched as their Russian fellows approached the Grand Prelate and knelt before him for his blessing and bent their heads before the fine shower of holy water.

The Grand Prelate turned his bearded face to the clergy of other nations, smiled at them, and lifted his hands.

"The Most Holy God has granted mercy to His daughter, Russia, and has accepted her penance," he said, in English.

Tears filled his old eyes as he continued in his strongly accented voice.

"Our people are free, and our churches are filled with our children. The government of our country implores all her sister nations to accept Russia into the brotherhood of man, into the fatherhood of God. You have prayed for us, and your prayers have been answered, and we have prayed, and our land is bright again and full of the laughter of free men." He clasped his hands together and chanted:

"My soul doth magnify the Lord, and my spirit hath rejoiced in God, my Savior!"